THE CHILL

Romano Bilenchi

THE CHILL

*Translated from the Italian
by Ann Goldstein*

Europa
editions

Europa Editions
116 East 16th Street
New York, N.Y. 10003
www.europaeditions.com
info@europaeditions.com

Copyright © by Romano Bilenchi Estate. All rights reserved
First Publication 2009 by Europa Editions

Translation by Ann Goldstein
Original title: *Il gelo*
Translation copyright © 2009 by Europa Editions

Library of Congress Cataloging in Publication Data is available
ISBN 978-1-933372-90-7

Bilenchi, Romano
The Chill

Book design by Emanuele Ragnisco
www.mekkanografici.com

Cover illustration by Emanuele Ragnisco

Prepress by Plan.ed – Rome

CONTENTS

THE CHILL

The chill of suspicion and incomprehension came between me and humankind when I was sixteen, at the time of my high-school exams. I had witnessed the drought, with both country and city dwellers overwhelmed, pressed against the soil from which the crops had retreated to the point of disappearing, and seen the roads disintegrate at the touch of fields now without perimeters, without hedges of hawthorn and bloodtwig, having become elongated piles of dust where farmers, animals, and field hands struggled to find any sign of fruit or plant or blade of grass; I had observed, in those days, earth and people raging, crazed, against the unbearable servitude imposed by heaven, and my family, acquiescent and vile, set themselves against my grandfather. But then one morning all the green of the plain, of the vineyards and the wooded hills, reemerged and flourished again; and I saw the inhabitants of the countryside make their farms more fertile than before, irrigate them more wisely, introduce into them new species of trees that pleased me, hazelnuts, for instance, and mulberries, with their fruit that first was white and then, little by little, took on a darker tinge. Nor did the ambiguous attitude of my parents leave any sediment in my soul; every trace of moral judgment and rancor disappeared with the first green budding on the plants in the garden and the fields.

Between the drought and the poverty had come the death of my grandfather, and I got over that grief, too, a laceration overflowing with anguish and bewilderment at how he had left me. But I hadn't been prey to desperate, dramatic outbursts, like my mother and grandmother, in spite of the love I felt for that man who was so different from the others, and whom I had defended, followed, and supported in all his exploits. I wasn't able to be there when my grandfather died, couldn't keep him company, talk to him in those last moments of his life, care for him. It was a Thursday morning in spring; there was no school, and we boys, led by our mathematics teacher, spent that day on our weekly long hike to the top of Monte Luca, the highest peak around, named for an old chapel standing right on the summit and dedicated to the apostle, now reduced to a shelter for woodcutters and charcoal burners—its small iron cross split by a lightning strike—and entangled, right up to its walls, which were covered with marks and inscriptions, by a thick, impenetrable brush and the branches of ilex and beech trees. We met in front of the school and, traversing the flat countryside along a road that followed the river for several kilometers, we reached a castle situated on a slope of the mountain. Its village and a few of the fortress walls remained intact, and we drank at a cistern in the middle of the courtyard. Racing to get there first, in order to pull up the bucket, we'd take off suddenly, in agreed-on twos or threes, from as far as two hundred meters away. One of us would grab the bucket and, protected by his companions and by the wall of the cistern behind him, spray water on the others mercilessly, summer or winter, as long as he had the strength and was not vanquished in a desperate assault by the boys who had been provoked. The small courtyard of the cistern was surrounded by a low stone wall now whitened by time: the professor, in class a harsh and demanding man, would sit on the wall, his gaze wandering over the ruins of the fortress or the uneven pavement of the courtyard, where the grass, emerging between stone and stone, had created for itself enormous spaces to grow; he let us fight until we were exhausted, and then we lay panting on the paving stones or sat on the wall, caressed sometimes in summer by a light wind that came to refresh us from behind the ruins of the ancient fortifications.

The professor had told us the history of the castle many times, from the count abbot and the Longobard lords to the era of the medieval communes, when it had become the outpost, in my homeland, of a city not far away and now in decline. Observing the professor, I thought I caught in his gaze, shifting constantly from the fortress walls to the courtyard, my own astonishment at a geography so undone—I would have liked to depend on that small ancient city, solid and mighty, that bore in its stones the traces of millennia of history—and at the dereliction of the men who had not prevented the castle's destruction, depriving me of heaven knows what resources for my imagination.

After our rest, we set off again on our climb up Monte Luca. Beyond the castle the road continued through a tall, cleared wood; in April it was bordered by cascades of dense, sweet-smelling hawthorn, and in May, beyond the hedge, by clumps of broom that created a gaudy disorder among the vegetation. The road was well maintained, smooth as a city street, and we met carriages, carts, men on mules, and even some trucks.

When we reached the chapel, we looked at the walls to see if there were new signatures and, if we found any, commented on them at length. Then, sitting on the ground in a circle, we waited for the professor's permission to open our knapsacks and eat. Afterward, we picked up the papers, piled them inside the chapel, and set them on fire; as soon as all the smoke had made its way out through the hole that someone had made in the roof just beside the little cross, we lay down amid the underbrush, arranged according to our friendships and affections, some leaning our heads against tree trunks, and rested for an hour. We talked with the professor about the history and the flora and fauna in these places; in another school in the city, which was a girls' school, he taught science, and, passionate about botany, knew the names of all the plants, their life cycles, their sudden appearance and disappearance from the earth, their powerful challenge to the ages.

He would sat on a big rock in our midst, his body erect, blue eyes behind gold-rimmed glasses, his curly, nearly blond, chestnut-brown hair loose on his forehead. There was a constant exchange of questions and answers between us and him. The vegetation on Monte Luca on the side we climbed was sparse, but he had told us that some hundred and fifty kilometers farther south was a mountain group that—clearly visible from a distance, because it was dark with chestnuts and oaks—rose up in a vast valley, pale gray because of the clay soil; in that mountainous area, with its ancient towns and villages, more than three hundred and fifty types of plants had been counted. Rich in water, it had once been equally rich in history, studded with castles and fortifications, and had a famous abbey, which was the destination of pontiffs, emperors, and kings, from King Racis

to Charlemagne, and where, in the centuries before the
year 1000, young priests came to study, even from Ger-
many, from cities like Mainz, making the incredible journey
on muleback. During all of our outings, we talked about
the mountain, about the plants that thrived there, about the
Longobards and the warrior abbots; the rest hour passed
quickly, and, our minds dazed with what the professor had
told us and went on telling us, we set off for home. We
went back by a different route than the one we had come
by, it, too, clear and smooth, going down another face of
the mountain: quieter and more solitary, thickly wooded,
and a little gloomy, partly because of the darkness that, the
sun having long since set, penetrated it, began, near the valley floor, to blur the contours of the already dense under-
growth, and the trunks of the trees. At the foot of the
mountain, the road skirted an ancient abbey, once on the
edge of vast, tenacious marshes surrounding a lake of vol-
canic origin, reclaimed centuries and centuries earlier by
hundreds of monks.

Unlike the castle, the abbey still offered conspicuous,
secure pegs for our fantasies of olden times: two churches,
one very small, of gray stone; the guesthouse that must
once have been bathed by the marsh waters; a long, low
brick structure containing monks' cells that, on one side,
flanked a cloister as big as a town square and untraversa-
ble because of the red dust of the crumbled bricks; and,
opposite the still intact colonnade, immense storage rooms
that the inhabitants of the few houses situated on the other
side of the road had made into coal cellars. But what most
amazed us boys were the still solid, high perimeter walls,
ornamented, every twenty meters or so, by potbellied towers whose every slit bore traces of liquid tar, and the still

functioning drawbridge over a deep moat that the farmers and the priest, who lived in the abbey, in a small house next to a church, kept clear of nettles, weeds, and rocks.

It was still early, and, without pressure of time, we divided into equal sides, elected the abbot and the Longobard count, appointed foot soldiers and knights, and began the battle on the drawbridge. In order to win, the band that was outside the walls had to penetrate the broad courtyard; anyone captured by the defenders became their prisoner and, under the guard of one of the adversaries, had to stay put inside one of the coal cellars, on his honor not to escape. The bridge and its neighboring towers, deserted and for centuries immured, utterly aloof, even from the meager life of the countryside, were animated by the clamor of sounds and voices. The professor, having made sure that none of us were holding a rock, an oak branch, or a hawthorn bough, took a short walk on the plain toward some country shop or a house where the farmers kept sheep and had set aside some fresh cheese for him. Upon his return, having surveyed the position of the two sides, the ground lost by one or the other, he decided which should be assigned the victory. Having obediently accepted the verdict, we set off, on a path sunk so deep in the fields it seemed a canal, toward the provincial road that, leaving the mountain behind, brought us into the city near the riverbank.

I wouldn't have given up that weekly outing for anything. I was quiet, studious, not much inclined to friendship with boys of my age or disposed to take part in games except with the few close friends I had; of these, two were schoolmates and lived on the same street as me, one was an assistant clerk employed in a wholesale fabric business,

and the other the son of a carpenter who was already help-
ing his father, working in the shop, and who every day confided to us, in his anxiety about perfection and about
poverty to be vanquished only through work, the progress
he had made with the difficult and dangerous tools. These
were friendships that had arisen long ago through mutual
sympathy in the classroom or on the athletic field during a
soccer game. Otherwise, my family's affairs, my grandfather's ventures, my own imagination, capable on the slightest pretext of transforming our small garden into an
immense forest populated by elephants, equatorial birds,
fierce beasts—these were enough to fill the hours that
were not devoted to school and study.

And yet the Thursday outing transformed me: all my
schoolmates became friends for that day, and the professor, with whom in class it was impossible to maintain a
relationship that was not purely scholastic, became a culti-
vated and pleasant companion who was able to satisfy,
with the most pertinent details, our curiosity and our
desire to know. I became as rowdy and boisterous as the
strongest, the most quick-tempered and mischievous, with
tricks and inventions that my companions could never
anticipate and found it hard to counter, so that I was once
elected Longobard count and once abbot. In winter I
would conceal colds and slight influenzal fevers in order
not to miss the outing. If it rained, we would put off the
walk, and the tedium that flattened city and country irre-
sistibly assailed my mind as well, which with great effort
managed to formulate restorative fancies.

When we climbed Monte Luca we usually left the city
at eight in the morning and made our return at around
seven in the evening. One Thursday morning at six, grand-

mother waked my mother and me; grandfather had felt ill during the night, had groaned for hours, had talked about his Sicilian nephew, about his own Longobard origins, and had fallen asleep only to wake shortly afterward and recite a poem, invented on the spot, about the house cat and me—we, the cat and I, armed with guns, were going to a distant town to commit crimes, in particular, to steal the wallet of a friend of his. Because of grandfather's advanced age, grandmother was frightened and had come to consult us. I was sent to fetch the doctor, a wise old man, and a friend of the family, who for decades had known everything about us and sometimes treated us without coming to examine us, staying in his office reading novels and history books.

I found him already dressed, sitting in the living room drinking coffee, and he came with me immediately. On the way he said, "It can't be arteriosclerosis—I played cards with him two days ago. Your grandfather isn't sick, it's just that he's too old: that's what worries me. Some day or other he might suddenly go out, like a candle burning down to the end: he'll go because he's used up."

I trembled: although I knew that death existed in the world, always ready to appear—a few days before, a student in my class had died of meningitis—I didn't want my grandfather to leave me. As at the time of the drought, it seemed to me impossible that he was the same as others. He was healthy, I had never even heard him sneeze; and now he was leading an orderly life, between his reading, the café, and bed. Every year, in the summer, he went to take the hot baths, and he always sent me the same gray-blue postcard showing a hot-air balloon anchored in a square of the nearby town.

The doctor had grandmother tell him how grandfather had spent the preceding days. Apart from the continuous, obsessive idea about his distant descent from a Longobard count who centuries ago stopped in Lombardy and then advanced into the center of our peninsula in the train of Cillane, leader of the Tuscia—an interest that had never reached the height of his passion for the farm: both innocent infatuations, even grandmother said, that served to pass the time—grandfather had not in the slightest changed his habits. He had written to his nephew in Palermo asking him to have some research done on the family's heraldic past. After a month, a coat of arms had arrived for him, bearing a crest with red and blue feathers and this inscription: "Citing the Commendatore Giovan Battista di Crollalanza in his historical heraldic dictionary of noble and notable families, we find this family, originally from Piedmont. They were lords of Piobesi."

Between the lords of Piobesi and Cillane's paladin, grandfather was puzzled. He had asked me and my mother, who had had almost enough schooling to become a teacher, what we knew about the Longobards; he wanted us to read him what was written in my schoolbook and in those that mamma had kept and that, according to him, must include the results of the most recent historical research. He was silent when my mother told him that the Longobards were both barbarian and Germanic. A Pope, Gregory I, my book said, spoke of them in his *Dialogues* as "a savage people" who advanced over our bodies, and added, "Empty and deserted now is our land, and no one inhabits it." The invasion had been a scourge for northern and central Italy: houses and churches sacked, lands seized, and dead everywhere.

Grandfather wanted us to repeat for him how Agilulfo, the duke of Turin, had conquered Italy, how King Rotari had seized Genoa. He sought details on the conquest of Lucca and on the counts of Donoratico, cities quite near ours; but my mother and I knew only what the history books reported, and the readings that followed the account of the facts. There were some bibliographical notes, but they referred to old books, not available to us or to grandfather. Finally, since Agilulfo was the duke of Turin, and Turin and Piobesi were in Piedmont, he said he was sure that the coat of arms, the genealogical tree, and history coincided: he was descended from a family of Longobard nobles.

Grandmother looked at him with a smile, shook her head, and said to him that he and his father had owned large stores selling various goods, both retail and whole-sale, and that he had separated from the family in order to live independently, and had opened a hotel. As far as she knew, as far as everyone in town knew, his had been a family devoted to commerce for generations. Nowhere near the likes of Cillane, Agilulfo, and Piobesi. Since grandfather became agitated and begged her not to meddle in his affairs, she said to him that when people get old they go back to being children, and that he should go ahead and pursue those origins that were lost in time. In fact she was happy about it, this way he wouldn't get into trouble.

I condemned grandmother's attitude, because, although appreciating it in many ways, I could find in it only pity and even contempt. From my history teacher and from books, I had learned that in our country invasions had succeeded one another endlessly, devastating countryside and city. I thought that the origins of a family could be verified merely for some hundreds of years. What had happened before that no one could know, and it didn't seem strange to me that there were those who had among their distant ancestors a Longobard—or Norman, or French, or Saracen—prince.

The doctor checked grandfather's reflexes, exchanged a few words with him about an event of years earlier, the escape of a horse on our street one market day, and immediately said, "From that point of view he's fine, as I imagined. Acute arteriosclerosis is manifested by other symptoms: you don't even recognize the people you live with anymore, and you also become mean. The Longobards have nothing to do with it. If there's no trouble in his chest, he's still a healthy man. Sometimes even a young person can be suffering from severe pneumonia that doesn't cause a fever and is difficult to hear when you're listening to his breathing."

Grandfather, his head still adorned with thick white curls, looked attentively at the doctor and smiled. He had taken off his nightshirt; he had a fleshy chest, the skin still young and smooth. The doctor had listened to it and, shaking his head, said, "I really don't find anything." He made grandfather get up, palpated his whole body, and again listened to his chest. "Usual smoker's catarrh, especially on the lower right." After examining grandfather's eyes with the help of a pocket flashlight, he asked him to follow with his gaze a finger that he moved rapidly in front of his eyes. The small thermometer showed a normal temperature. Then the doctor asked what food grandfather had eaten the night before and, having found out, scolded him as if he were a child: "At our age you should get up from the table hungry, especially after dinner."

Grandmother had tried to bring the conversation back to the state of grandfather's mind, but the doctor replied, "The fact that he talks about the Longobards and recites a poem about the cat when he's half asleep means nothing. Many people have fixations. At eighty we don't have the mind of a man of thirty. It might have been a momentary confusion. The important thing is that organically there is nothing wrong. And that I'm sure of." Finally he told us not to worry: he would be back in the afternoon.

I had asked him if I could go with my schoolmates to Monte Luca, and he, smiling, had answered that not only could I but I should: the purpose was physical health, and the stronger I got as a boy the better off I would be as an old man. Health was based on the two "M"s: moderation and movement. That night, the doctor assured me, I would find grandfather as youthful and strong as the day before. He would recover in a few hours. The doctor prescribed drops for his heart and a vegetable-based laxative and left.

I immediately rushed to the meeting place for the outing. Most of my companions were there, waiting for the few latecomers. At first I wasn't as eager and cheerful as the others; I was distracted, seemingly incapable of freeing myself from the stupor that leaves a stubborn drowsiness, and I was unable to join in the conversations and songs, or pay attention to what our mathematics teacher was saying. Then that fog disappeared, and in its place I found a biting anxiety about grandfather.

Now his insistence on his noble and Longobard ancestors seemed strange to me, too, as did the adventures I supposedly had with the cat. The abrupt awakening, grandmother's story, grandfather so calmly leaning against the pillow, his white curls scattered around his head, his incredibly youthful naked body seemed to me almost dramatic.

I refused the position of aide to the leader of the Longobards; I joined in the fight, but without enthusiasm. As we descended from the mountaintop, the road was darker than usual, with the mist beginning to rise among vegetation still damp from the rain of the day before. We met a dark-haired, dark-skinned girl with a surly, hard look, who was fiercely whipping the young mule that carried her. With every step of the beast, the girl's legs lifted and lowered, hitting the mule's stomach convulsively. She was wearing a dress of a pink-and-blue striped fabric that the old women of the mountains wove, along with wool-and-cotton cloth, on the slow winter days. When we encountered her she kept looking straight ahead and, paying no attention to us, went on singing a little song, in which she inveighed against another girl, Carla, of whom she was jealous, calling her the relative of a yellow squash, with skin like a lemon peel, and eyes as gruesome as an owl's.

"I wouldn't want to be that Carla," Lino said, but no one laughed. We stopped talking; our little groups drew close and our silence placed a heavy seal on the already absolute silence of the wood. I looked at the professor; the girl's spitefulness seemed to have struck him, too. His body of an adult man had grown thin, his small eyes had turned glassy. We didn't start talking again until we came in sight of the abbey.

When I got home I found that grandfather had died. Mamma and grandmother told me that at midday grandfather had been seized by a sudden delirium. He had got up from the bed and, wearing only his long nightshirt and brandishing his walking stick, had gone to the end of the garden, where, thrashing the hedges and the wall, he shouted that the barbarians would not harm him, would not seize his farm in the hills—not remembering, as grandmother said, that he hadn't owned the farm for a long time. The first-floor tenants had hurried out and with their help mamma and grandmother had tried to get him into bed. With his back against the wall, he had threatened to beat everyone. Over and over he exclaimed, "The time has come to go. I must go. I am going." Then he calmed down and they led him to his room, holding him by the hand.

The doctor had visited him again, without finding anything new. He stayed at his bedside for more than an hour, but grandfather, now quiet, answered all his questions as if nothing had happened, in fact he didn't remember a single detail of his flight into the garden. The doctor had recommended making him eat light, nutritious food, prescribing a sedative so that he would sleep as long as possible. He added that he should be watched, not left alone for a moment. Grandfather had asked only for a consommé, saying that his stomach hurt. And he had gone to sleep.

Because his room was at the end of the hall, far from the kitchen and the living room, mamma and grandmother had asked an old woman who lived nearby to keep grandfather company. He woke around four in the afternoon and, very lucid—his mind filled with memories of his youth and that of the old woman, whom he had known since she was a girl—had begun to joke with her, reminding her of long-ago loves, of when she, who had been very beautiful, had enjoyed flirting with more than one boy at a time. They had given him another cup of broth, which he had drunk greedily; then, turning on his side, his face hidden from the old woman, he had fallen asleep again. A little later, while my companions and I were starting back toward the city, mamma had tried to wake him to give him something else to eat but he hadn't answered. They had called to him in loud voices, caressed his head and then shaken his arm. Grandfather died in his sleep, peacefully, without expressing a wish, or saying a word, either for me or for the others.

Grandfather had expired a short time before I rang at the house door. Mamma was kneeling at the foot of the bed, crying; grandmother, beside the night table, her body bent forward, was gazing, astonished, at grandfather's calm face. I went to hug my mother, and wept with grief, but not as I would have wept if I had been present at his death. I was sure that dying in his sleep, without suffering and without being noticed by the others and perhaps without expecting it himself, was an end worthy of him. I recalled the long periods of torpor that had assailed that hefty, heavy body before he'd bought the farm: those, too, were times when he could have one day suddenly crossed from life into death.

Besides, it was in grandfather's company that I had conceived my first thoughts of death, had begun to meditate on the mystery of it and the various ways we can meet it on our path. Not long before, grandfather had taken me to visit a friend of his, the director of a wealthy museum in a very ancient city near ours: as children they had been together in nursery school and then at elementary school; years later, when grandfather opened the hotel, his friend had stayed there during an entire season of archeological excavations that were being carried out near a town in our province.

When we arrived at the museum, the director was not in his office; the guard told us he was supervising the excavation of a small Roman amphitheater that, by chance, had been discovered two weeks earlier outside the city walls, barely a kilometer from the museum. We went there immediately. Capitals and columns, quite short, and some statues, were sticking up out of an enormous circular pit dug in the earth. At the edge of the pit, with his back to the countryside, at the base of the steep slope of the hill on which the city stood, and which then plunged down to a narrow valley spotted with clayey earth, was the director. He was a tall, thin man, well dressed and distinguished-looking, with a heavy gold chain across his vest. Every so often he took his hand out of his pocket and gestured to four workmen, who were digging with hoes and spades, not to strike too violently.

Grandfather and the director embraced and kissed each other on the cheek. It was an autumn afternoon and, because of the light but constant wind and the altitude, the air was cold, as if it were the start of winter. After the greeting, the director began to pay greater attention to what the workmen were doing. The wind grew stronger, more sporadic, came in gusts and whipped our bodies, the earth, the ruins, the walls that, built of solid blocks of stone, rose just before us. The director went down into the pit, knelt on a mound of earth, combed through it with his hands, and, obliging the workers to move slowly and prudently, uncovered the statue of an athlete with one arm raised above his head. He returned to us and said, "One crack of the hoe or spade would have been enough to cut off the head or a shoulder."

In spite of the cold, grandfather and I stayed to watch

the digging for two more hours, until the work day was over. A few minutes before we left, a worker hit an obstacle with his hoe. We heard a sharp blow, like the clash of two pieces of iron. Grandfather's friend again hurried into the pit and, working partly with his hands, partly with a mason's trowel, pulled a marble head out of the dirt, its nose just severed by the hoe. It represented a young man with a tuft of hair on his forehead and a mournful, desolate gaze: the whole face had a poignant delicacy. After looking at it for a long time the director said, "It must be a portrait of Augustus as an adolescent. At around eighteen he suffered a long illness. You see this dazed, dreamy, pained look. It reveals a young man stricken by with a preoccupation that saddens him." He told one of the workers to take it to the museum; he would clean it and display it in a room there. "I'll also have an expert in Roman art look at it, but I'm sure I'm not mistaken. It's an important discovery," he said. After a while he added, "Just a few more minutes and we'll go." He didn't seem to feel the cold.

At that point three of the workers said goodbye, got on their bicycles, and slowly passed through an open gate in the wall a short distance from us. The fourth stayed to dig under the statue of the athlete, which was lying face up on the ground. Suddenly, from underneath the statue, he drew out a small leather pouch closed with a tie, also of leather, like the one grandfather kept his tobacco in. In great excitement, the worker ran toward us and stretching out his arm offered it to the director, who exclaimed with pleasure and astonishment. Undoing the tie, he took from the pouch some Roman coins. He said that someone, perhaps a young man, had lost it in the amphitheater; it was strange that no one had picked it up, and who could say why it had remained there for centuries, as if the theater had suddenly collapsed on people enjoying a performance, a gladiatorial contest, perhaps. And yet from history there was no report of a disaster striking the city, as had happened at Pompeii and Herculaneum, where such discoveries were common.

Grandfather and the director began talking about the barbarian invasions, and the Longobards, but grandfather did not refer to the hypothesis of his own possible Longobard descent in front of his friend. Maybe the theater really had been destroyed right at the time when the barbarians invaded. We looked for a long time at the pouch, handing it back and forth, and felt the coins, which seemed almost new, if a little darkened. "They're coins of the late empire," the director said. "I'll study them carefully."

Grandfather said that it was time to go, and, accompanied by his friend, we went to the square where the bus stopped. Taking leave of us, the director said, "Today, dear friends, we have seen death, we have seen how precarious our existence is, and who can say if we will leave even a coin purse as a relic of our time on earth. Countless generations of men have succeeded one another since then. Every New Year's Day, it seems to me that the world with its seasons is starting out on a journey, and I'm sucked into a vortex, imagining that, this very year, I might suddenly get off the train and find myself in an unknown station from which it is impossible to go on."

Turning to me he said, "Contrary to what many people think, awareness of the transient is what gives value to a man's life. In a great amphitheater in southern Italy, I saw friends dumbstruck at the sight of a brick that was still intact, with its maker's mark on it, and turn pale on seeing the room where the gladiators waited before rushing into the arena. The walls were covered with signatures in Thracian and other unknown languages. My friends declared that it was pointless to live when everything had already been done, consumed. But it's not true; one after another, toward a grand event, one generation constructs the roads on which the new ones travel, as a Chinese proverb says."

Now, in the presence of grandfather's body, so intact and serene, I was sure that he had left much more than a Roman purse containing a few ancient coins. Between us a deep trust had been established, and a new, boundless love, not tinged by any sadness.

Unexpectedly, thanks to the experience he had acquired in his profession, my father was offered the opportunity to return to us. The owner of a paper mill died, and the widow and her children, although emotionally attached to the father's work and fairly experienced in the running of the business, were not able to deal with the complexity of the unpredictable things that, from one day to the next, could happen, the normal caprices of commerce. The woman, who had met my father and appreciated his abilities, asked him to manage the company. He would be home in a few months. Just at that time, as a little hope began to resurface in our house, grandmother received a small inheritance, which, with the impending return of my father, was another good sign. It came to her from a relative who had always lived alone and whom we seldom saw.

One morning, Pietro, a nephew of grandfather's, a bachelor, came to our house; he was influential in the city, because he had held sensitive public offices without leaving behind complaints or gossip. With a brother, Antonio, also a bachelor, he managed a small factory that produced a few types of winter fabric, made from a heavy soft wool that was sought after in neighboring cities as well, because it protected against the dampness that for months and months saturated the broad, long valley where ours was the most important city. The factory had about ten workers. It appeared to be profitable, since the two owners lived comfortably, kept two maids, and, many in the city declared, devoted to the table their more excessive desires. Pietro did the shopping, and the citizens could appreciate his lavishness.

No one had ever said anything bad about their private life, which was always under scrutiny. That day, though, Pietro told grandmother that Antonio had a lover who was costing him a lot of money, and that he and his brother were about to fail. Besides, our valley had been stricken by an anthrax epidemic that had killed almost all the sheep: and, since we were distant from the wealthier regions, and the cost of transport was very high, the situation was about to become impossible. The small companies were the ones that were suffering most; profit margins had been getting smaller from year to year, and now every length of material that came out of the factory cost more to make than what it sold for. Pietro, however, said he was sure that with a little new capital—which the banks had denied him, because they, alone in the city, knew the true state of his and Antonio's affairs—he would be able to modernize in one or two areas, come up with some new, less costly fabrics, and recover. Weeping, he asked grandmother to lend him the money that she had got from her inheritance. Along with a modest loan, he would have what he needed to remedy his affairs: if the bank gave her three per cent interest, he would pay up to ten and would soon restore to her the entire capital, which certainly was not large. He begged her to say nothing to my father.

My mother and grandmother, knowing him as a gentle man, and moved to pity by his look of a big, shy boy, who now seemed precociously aged, went immediately to the bank, withdrew the money, and gave it to Pietro. "Besides, it was an unexpected gift that we hadn't counted on. Father won't say anything, if he ever finds out," grandmother said. From that moment, Pietro began coming to our house often; he brought grandmother flowers, he was relaxed, sometimes gay, he recounted in abundant detail stories of the life he had led with his brother, he talked about women—subjects that seemed to me strange and not exactly edifying—and swore that his affairs had begun to improve. Suddenly, one day, Pietro died of a heart attack in a public urinal. He was found by a farmer who had come to town to the fair. Antonio declared bankrupt-cy: first he gave grandmother a part of the money she had lent them.

Meanwhile in the city all sorts of rumors spread about the two brothers, about their way of life, their eccentrici-ties, their passions, their management of the business. The rumors were sometimes banal, sometimes treacherous. A lawyer told grandmother that if she had valuable objects and expensive furniture she should hide them: she could be dragged into the failure as a de-facto partner in the busi-ness and everything she possessed could vanish in an instant, including the house. My grandmother and espe-cially my mother fell into despair, because the gossip also included the insinuation that mamma had been Pietro's lover. When we went out, people in shop entrances turned to glance at her quickly or stare at her and smile. There were also people who ostentatiously stopped to greet her, to offer consolation; but whether to vindicate her or cheer her up, they still had to utter some ugly words. I had been present at all the conversations between Pietro and my mother and grandmother, and I could have sworn in front of anyone that mamma had not enjoyed the more risqué talk, and had always been diffident and reserved. I was astonished, astounded, to the point where I didn't even think of rebelling, of attacking one of those people who stood sneering in the doorways of the shops. Above all, I was afraid of how my father would react when he returned.

The grief, the anger that had overwhelmed me at the time when grandfather bought the farm and drought burned the entire countryside, the desperation I had seen among the farmers, the torments of poverty that had wrapped around us like a terrifying snake, the widow's relentless tyranny were lost in a past so distant that I could not recover even its tiniest fragments. My feelings were a mire that was swallowing me up little by little. The thought that my neighbors, my fellow-townsmen, with whom I had often felt sympathy, could harbor such malice toward others, concealing it under an appearance of the opposite, annihilated me. I felt uncertain and spent.

I couldn't force myself to go beyond the outskirts of the city; I wandered through the streets, in the market, down the alleys, but everything seemed flat, houses, monuments, parks, everything became colorless. What I liked best in the city, besides my house, was Via dei Tre Mori, a long street that came from the countryside and grew more compact and more varied at the same time; the houses, mostly of the previous century, were solid, with large but never inelegant entrances, through which you could glimpse gardens with magnificent leafy plants or small, well-tended vegetable plots. The dark green of a medlar tree sometimes showed at the top of a wall. Most of the façades had bands of gray sandstone or travertine that made them more graceful. The street ended far away, in a spacious square, where above the rooftops you could see sprays of green, the highest branches of age-old trees.

Once I had stepped out of our front door, Via dei Tre Mori gave me the right thrust toward time. The façades, one against the next, gray, green, pink, ochre, inspired a peaceful, light serenity and pleasure, heightened by the green that I could see in the distance, touching the sky. I walked in tranquility between those reassuring walls: first I thought of the people who lived in the houses, near and far, that, gradually, I passed by, of placid hardworking families, where, at that moment, my friends who lived on the street might be. Even when I was melancholy or sad, the street, thanks to a ray of sunlight that struck a pink façade, a medlar tree, a window filled with flowers, would soothe me and make me happy again. But now I was almost afraid to go out. The other houses, it seemed to me, had their doors shut, as if to keep passersby at a distance, and the street was dark, almost as if it were about to announce, as once it had, one of those premonitory signs of drought that no one had wanted to recognize. If I sought a judgment my conscience lost its bearings.

At the time, I confided all my doubts and fears, my terror of what might happen when, a few days from now, my father returned, to Marco, my closest friend, a boy in my class, religious, on friendly terms with our parish priest, from whom he was learning Latin, but also lively and strong, always distinguishing himself during the outings to Monte Luca and the battles at the abbey, and often taking on the most prestigious military roles. Marco advised me to make a pilgrimage to another famous abbey, twenty kilometers from the city, in the opposite direction from the one at the foot of Monte Luca, where our battles took place. In olden times, as history and the traces of buildings demonstrated, it must have been an imposing complex, with lands extending through thick woods, through fields and swamps, as far as the sea. Immense architectural skeletons of its structures were still standing, exposed to the sun and storms: only one building, perpendicular to the entrance, was intact, habitable. It was part of the ancient refectory, with walls frescoed by illustrious painters; a few Dutch nuns lived there, drawn by the charm of the countryside. The remains, spread out on a knoll, amid a few stands of trees, allowed you to look out on meadows and fields, first encumbered with ruins and then grassy and green, some planted with grain and corn. To the left, a road parallel to the nearby provincial road led to a cupola-shaped structure; it was always open and held proof of a miracle that had taken place in the Middle Ages.

One night, a young man of libertine habits was returning home on horseback. He was overcome by sleep and the horse carried him, unaware, to that unfamiliar spot near the abbey. A voice said to him, "Abandon your depraved life. Stay here and begin a life as a hermit." Seeking proof that it was the voice of God, the young man answered, "If my sword pierces that rock I will obey." The sword penetrated the solid stone up to the hilt, and was still there, for visitors to see.

Marco had brought me to the abbey to pray at the pierced rock. Maybe peace would return to my family. We stopped near the refectory. My schoolmates and I, before we began going to Monte Luca, had explored the outskirts of the city in search of the best roads, the most suitable terrains. We had liked the abbey, for what the professor of mathematics explained to us one day about its distant past and for the way it looked in the present. In early times a river ran among the lower-lying structures; it drove a big mill, of which some stretches of wall remained, powered cloth factories, flowed past book binderies and storehouses of every kind. But it was not a place for outings, for ambushes, for battles: too many tall, bare columns. We gave it up reluctantly; it was a landscape to contemplate at length, sitting on the grass as Marco and I did that afternoon.

It was right at that time that my father returned home. He reproached grandmother for lending the money to Pietro, but reassured her that there was nothing to fear, even from the money returned by Antonio, because no receipts or other documents existed, and rumors were worth next to nothing. Pietro and Antonio's workers, from whom they had borrowed money and who now were left without jobs, came to consult with my father; but, aware of the honesty of the owners, they soon decided, following my father's advice, to wait for the bankruptcy procedure to take its course. In fact, it all worked out: the creditors, distressed by Pietro's death, which they attributed to his constant apprehensions, were satisfied to divide up the proceeds of the sale of the factory and the fabrics in the warehouses.

Mamma, in desperation, decided to tell father immediately what was being said about her in the city, and even called me as a witness of her innocence. But it seemed to me that my father already knew all about it: a sympathetic smile slightly altered his face. The more mamma defended herself, as if she were confronting her accusers one by one, the more father tried to calm her with allusions to a matter that would soon clarify her position. Indeed, the city had other things to talk about. A true, strange scandal stunned it, causing long-lasting vibrations of hilarity and disgust, and granting my mother a revenge that, even more grieved and surprised, she hadn't sought, or wanted.

The person who had started the rumor (it's not clear how my father had known about it from the start, even before returning to us) that mamma had been Pietro's lover was a teacher at my school who lived near us and had observed Pietro's comings and goings at our house. The woman was the wife of a doctor, one of the department chairmen at the hospital in the city. One day this doctor had examined a young, attractive woman, a Latin teacher at the high school, who was separated from her husband. He had fallen for the woman, and during his medical examinations had made awkward declarations of love. The teacher had rejected him with severity, with revulsion, considering him a hypocrite: he was always making a show of religious and moralistic sentiments.

The doctor had then begun to write her passionate love letters, anonymous, but in which he repeated the same words he had used during his examinations. Finally the woman, exasperated, handed over the letters to the principal of the school and the head of the hospital, so that they could form a judgment and prevent the doctor from con-

tinuing to importune her. She also sent copies of the letters
to the wife of the man who was in love with her. The affair
made for endless discussion in the houses, cafés, clubs,
theaters. There were those who swore, who wagered, that
in no other part of the world had anonymous love letters
like that ever been written. Ridicule followed the doctor
and his wife everywhere, and after a few days everyone had
forgotten the gossip about the relations between Pietro
and my mother.

During the first months that my father lived again in
Via dei Tre Mori, he worked tenaciously to master the
details of his new position, and tried to shore up the family's few assets. He managed to cancel the small mortgage
that weighed on our house, and, finally, to evict from the
first floor the tenants whom at one time we had had to
accept, and who had deprived us of the garden. In the
spring, helped by some farm workers, he spent days labor-
ing in the garden, straightening the paths, planting the
flower beds, taking down old trees that no longer bore
fruit, putting in new ones. From the first to the last instant,
I followed those swift, expert men who moved from place
to place, more to remedy the wrongs suffered by the earth,
its useless and cruel devastations, than to complete a task
whose execution was already settled and well known. The
men seemed to proceed randomly, but I realized that their
speed had an order, a geometric sense. In efficiency and
passion they surpassed even grandfather when he bought
the farm in the hills and transformed it, from moment to
moment, astonishing those who watched, and leaving my
mind, at night, full of colors that superimposed themselves
on one another, sometimes at an unbearable pace.

When the garden was back in order—more luxuriant

than before, though cleared of so many plants, and more modern, with other plants that promised splendid flowers and fruit—grandmother stopped going to work at the widow's shop. Father advised her to give it up gradually, as if it had been taken on not as a commitment but as a favor for a friend, which, because of other incumbent duties, she was no longer able to perform. In the early days of father's return, when the work in the garden had just begun, the widow and her daughter came to our house often, even twice a day. They wore clinging, sleeveless dresses, and the widow would not leave father, or even the workmen, for a moment; she talked—laughing, her mouth open—about everything, about the work, about my future marriage to her daughter. My mother did not seem to suffer from that merciless attention, as though she had done some wrong to father and had to make up for it; but she treated the woman coldly, even if she was never impolite. My father barely seemed to notice her.

One day, without any warning, the widow said that she was getting married, she was selling the shop and moving to another city. I noticed that mamma was glad about this decision, and I was pleased, but I expected that she would show her feelings, if timidly: yet some quiet arguments at night after dinner between grandmother and mother, above all about the widow's future, plunged the house even deeper into a strange atmosphere of apathy, which had arisen after the departure of the tenants and the restoration of the garden. I myself now saw those immediate initiatives as events too long awaited to contain anything new. Grandfather, the drought, the widow, Pietro and Antonio were too far removed, almost as if they hadn't existed. Every night father withdrew to the study that had been grandfather's and not the slightest movement could be heard, or he returned to the factory or went with friends to the café.

Again I perceived obscure signs of unease. But one afternoon, coming out of the house, I found Via dei Tre Mori full of lights, festive. I was on my way to ask Marco for advice again, propose a return to the abbey and the rock pierced by the sword of the saint. Abruptly I turned back, went to mamma and grandmother and asked if I could invite my school friends to our house, including the ones I had been in the school play with, so they could see how free and welcoming our house had become again, how spacious and orderly the garden. Mamma and grandmother, as if they had expected nothing else, agreed; I wanted them to get father's permission; they said it wasn't necessary, father was never home, and in any case they would take care of what was needed. They promised to prepare drinks and sweets.

My friends and schoolmates received the invitation happily, and they all came as though we saw each other every day, the way we used to. Unexpectedly, father came home; many of them scarcely knew him even by sight, and he asked kindly about their families, the business and occupations of their fathers. On Sunday, three days later, he got me up early and took me to the country; we went as far as the hills where grandfather had had his farm. Father let me show him the boundaries. The farmer who had then lived there still did, helped on the land by his son, who, before grandfather gave up the farm, had been barely bigger than me; now he appeared a tall, robust young man. The farmer recognized me, though he made no allusion to grandfather and the drought, and invited me to pick some ripe fruit. I saw all the trees again, all growing in the same place as before; nothing really new was under cultivation.

There came a terrible year: an abrupt, short autumn, a very cold winter, a spring in which the flowers didn't bloom or immediately withered. Endless days, almost always spent in the house through autumn and winter, quickly dissipated past and even recent time; grandfather's fight against the drought, the atrocious, sticky period of poverty that had submerged us, the tragic failure of Pietro and Antonio suddenly dissolved, and even the details, so violent and clear, vanished; out of them rose people's faces, grandfather, grandmother, mamma, Pietro and Antonio— serious masks, fleshy, oppressive. With my father's return and the trip to the country it had seemed to me that I had got past those painful tests which life had imposed on us. Instead, a subtle chill unexpectedly came over me, when- ever my imagination placed before me images of the peo- ple with whom my existence was entwined: sometimes I became uneasy even at the thought of my classmates, the boys I saw every day. I feared the slightest change that might interfere with our inclinations.

The professor of mathematics was transferred to a dis- tant city, beyond our valley; and the outings to Monte Luca, the battles at the abbey ceased. Habits altered, as if our tastes, our interests had been determined by that kind and cultured man. Some of us withdrew to a more restricted life, chose other friends, other pastimes. I found myself left with those strange chill hours, having failed to store up either defenses or offensives for separating from the others and joining the more independent and daring. I finally found a small group; we played soccer, and around six in the evening we would end up at my house, studying—three boys, Marco, Lino, and I, and three girls, Rosa, Giovanna, and Susa. I was diligent, smart, and I helped the others, but my thoughts, my actions were always floating on a magma that hadn't hardened, and that might, in who knew what direction, start flowing again.

One day, under a low sky of a tenuous blue, as I was about to reach the soccer field, more caught up in observing the circling of a falcon intent on hunting down a small bird than in the actions of my companions, I lost an envelope of foreign stamps that I was going to paste that evening in the album that held my collection. Many boys at school collected stamps, mainly because we discovered in them images of exotic, mysterious countries that we would never have thought had mail service: the geography books showed photographs of savage, naked men, even cannibals, in the midst of tigers, elephants, and other animals, big and small, strange. My envelope was folded in four, bulging, blue. When I realized I had lost it, I asked my friends if they had seen it. Inside were four series of Asian and African stamps that no other boy in the city had. While I was looking around the field and along the edge where I had been watching the falcon's maneuvers, a boy came up to me and said that Marco—the friend who had suggested the pilgrimage to the abbey to obtain the grace that so mattered to me—had taken the stamps: there was no doubt, he had shown them a little earlier to a friend of his. I looked for Marco and asked for the stamps, but he denied having found them. That night I went to his house and forced him to give them to me, threatening to tell his father, an honest, gruff shopkeeper who would not hesitate to use the belt on him. I got the stamps, but our friendship was over. Even though I promised not to say anything, Marco stopped coming to my house to study, and I was never able to give my friends a convincing, sincere explanation for his absence. I couldn't understand what had happened—Marco's feelings and actions, how I had behaved. I broke into a cold sweat whenever I recalled the moment I had demanded the stamps, or had gone to his house to threaten him. It seemed to me that, of the two of us, I was the more guilty, and I felt almost afraid, and couldn't even look at him, when I met him on the street.

With Lino, the other friend who studied with me, I decided one day to raise a brood of finches. We went to the farmer who worked the farm that had been grandfather's. The man knew of a nest of finches, and he brought us to see it. Suspended not too high up in a sapling at the end of a row of vines, it was like a ball of grayish straw, compact and silent. The farmer, holding us around the waist, lifted us up with great care, and in the nest we could see four immobile, featherless birds, eyes closed. The man told us to return after twenty days; then the birds would be able to eat by themselves, without the help of their parents, and could live in a cage. Early in the afternoon of the agreed-on day, Lino went alone to the farmer and, with the excuse that I was sick and couldn't come, had the man give him the finches. He brought them home and kept them to raise on his own. In vain I begged him to give me just one, since I so much wanted it. He stubbornly refused, and I became almost crazed; little by little Lino stopped talking to me. Suddenly Lino and Marco united against me, and persuaded our girl friends not to study at my house anymore; at school they constantly sowed doubts about how smart I was, said that my best papers had been written by my mother, that my grandfather had been mad and I would be, too, when I grew up. They went to such extremes in harassing me, destroying my things, ruining my clothes, that the Latin teacher, having discovered them tearing the collar of my raincoat, reported them to the principal and had them suspended. Pointing to me as the voluntary cause of their punishment, they even quit the soccer team we played on.

More and more, I felt rejected by those I knew, and moments of isolation were frequent. The most painful sensation was one that hit me at night when I went to bed: I felt a sharp certainty that I was not as strong as others, was incapable of defending myself, of asserting myself, of alighting under the wings of those existences who, in their tranquil flight, seemed to cover all and make them equal, natural, and happy, whatever adversity befell them.

My only remaining friends were Alberto, the assistant clerk, and Nicola, the carpenter's son, both of whom worked in shops on Via dei Tre Mori. I kept them talking as long as possible when I met them: one day, as if aware of the solitude that was working its way ever more deeply into me, they invited me to join their soccer team. Very soon Alberto was entrusted with more difficult and responsible tasks: he had to maintain relations with certain factories, go to the bank; his free time diminished in the evening he left the shop late, and gradually he assumed the habits of a grownup. He became reserved and started going to the shopkeepers' café, where he clung to his employer and his son, eager to talk about business. Even on Sundays, he wouldn't come on walks with Nicola and me. He preferred some young men a bit older than he, who had welcomed him into their group, not numerous but enterprising, and went with them to see soccer matches in neighboring cities.

Since I was always with Nicola, I had confided to him all my weaknesses, my suspicions, fears. I even confessed to him that I loved Rosa, one of the girls who used to study at my house. She was a year older than me and we were in the same class. We were often together, separate from the others. Sometimes she was sick, so I let her copy my Italian compositions and our other homework, and every day I told her what happened at school, what the students said, the professors, how the recitations went. Often she would ask if a friend or a teacher was wearing something new, and I observed everything carefully in order to please her. I was very fond of her, I couldn't help being near her as much as possible, stopping by her house at least once a day, in the late afternoon. Her relatives—her mother had died when Rosa was small—were very kind to me and encouraged me to come and see her, to study with her. I thought that when I was older I would become engaged to her, marry her. At school, too, my companions said this openly and no one interrupted us, coming to ask me for information, advice. One day, I found out that Rosa, though still a teenager, had got engaged to a young shopkeeper, older than she and very rich: an aunt of Rosa's, whom I ran into on the street, confirmed this, and with a hard look on her face that did not admit complaint or remonstrance told me that Rosa would be getting married as soon as she finished school. When I asked Rosa if it was true, if she had secretly made this agreement with a stranger, she said that we could go on studying together as before, that we could always see each other, that nothing would change between us: but I, desperate and disappointed, because I'd imagined that Rosa had the same feelings for me as I had for her, and believing myself betrayed, refused. I would not be at school for much longer in my city, I would do my homework alone, I would talk and walk only with Nicola. At the end of our conversation it seemed to me that Rosa was looking at me with astonishment, with condescension, as if I were a child. The chill that stabbed me in the back like a knife made me stammer. I felt that she dominated me, was more adult, stronger, like Lino when he stole the finches.

Sometime later, on a Sunday, I saw Rosa arm in arm with her fiancé: they were walking along a shady street parallel to Via dei Tre Mori, one of those favored by young couples who, segregated from the larger public, compared their looks and their clothes. The man seemed even stronger and taller: Rosa, still a fragile child, awkward, her narrow shoulders squared and bent forward, had lost the customary movements that often gave her an air of assurance and ease and grace. Maybe she, too, was gripped by the chill that was blocking me. Nicola was walking beside me. I grabbed him by a sleeve and dragged him away. When we got home I poured out my sorrow. Nicola suffered with me and devised plans to break up Rosa's new union. He imagined a cruel revenge. For years and years, I remembered that day of anguish. A short while later, Nicola went to talk to Rosa. She confessed to him that one of her aunts had pushed her to become engaged to the wealthy young man. To Nicola, Rosa seemed very changed, frivolous; she considered me someone with an unstable, overcomplicated character. She said that she had always thought I liked one of our schoolmates—Lia, the daughter of the owner of a small café.

Nicola came back indignant at her lie and from that day on avoided her.

Nicola had an eighteen-year-old sister named Anna, who attended a girls' school in a nearby city, where, every morning, she went by bus. Anna was one of the most beautiful girls in my city, and her father and brother, who worked hard, indulged her with clothes and trinkets. Men already looked at her with desire, and many young men had asked her to get engaged. Anna was tall and had a good figure, and a round, calm face; she avoided the looks and the compliments with a sweet, serious smile, and to the question of marriage said that she would think about it when she had finished her studies. Now, by going to school, she had to repay the privations and sacrifices that her father and brother endured for her every day.

One Sunday morning, as I was standing in the square at the end of Via dei Tre Mori with some boys who, every week, gathered at the newspaper kiosk—it was well supplied with adventure magazines, which we would buy and then, to save money, exchange—Anna passed by. "Who could have imagined," said one of the boys, "that Anna would let herself be screwed by Luigi." We all laughed, the coupling seemed so improbable. Luigi was a strange character: a man of around fifty, stupid and vain, who often stood in front of the big mirror in the café or a shop window to gaze at himself, stroking his face and neatening his hair. He would smile in satisfaction. The whole town knew that his wife would betray him for money with anyone who asked. He was known for a joke played on him by Giuseppe, a blacksmith, a man over sixty, who spent the whole day playing cards. One night, when the café was full of people, the smith had called to Luigi and had given him some money, saying, "Take this to your wife; she lent it to me a few days ago. Just tell her: this is from Giuseppe." Then, when Luigi was gone, he told everyone that the money was the price agreed on for an hour in bed with Luigi's wife. The story was repeated everywhere, from café to café, shop to shop, house to house. When a man lived without any apparent income, people used to say, "He must be like Luigi, he manages his wife's career." The boy insisted that Anna was going with Luigi, and we, especially me, told him to stop; it was an absurd joke that would, if it got around, be harmful to Anna. The boy became serious and agitated. "Everyone knows it," he said. "Everyone except you." "Supposing for a moment that it's true, they certainly can't have been the ones who spread it," said another boy. "But how do they do it, where have they been together—in the middle of a field?" "I'll explain," said the boy who had spoken first. "Every morning when she goes to school, she leaves on the bus that arrives an hour before classes, and she gets off before she reaches the city. Luigi waits for her at the stop outside Porta Romana. From there they go to an inn that's not too far away—the owner is a friend of Luigi's." Another boy, the oldest among us, wriggled like a belly dancer and shouted. "Imagine what licking and all the rest. Only idiots get lucky," he said; and, as if he couldn't stand his own images, he fled. "How did you know?" another boy asked the one who had so unexpectedly mentioned Anna's affair. "My father told my mother. It seems that Luigi himself, to show off, talked about it to Bruno, the man who manages the café at the sports club. And when Bruno made fun of him, saying he'd made the whole thing up, Luigi, conceited as ever, showed him letters from Anna, where she recalled the sensations she'd had in their hours at the inn. Bruno, in turn amazed by what he'd heard and read, told his friends about Luigi's passions."

Gathered around the kiosk we could hardly believe this talk, which to some of us seemed insane. An argument arose and soon, to impose our own opinions, we began shouting. It was winter, and we were standing in a sunny corner behind the kiosk; two or three of us had our backs to the square. It was one of these who gave the alarm: Nicola emerged headlong from around the kiosk and stopped in the middle of the group. I had the impression that he had heard the last words. "I've been looking for you," he said to me breathlessly. Then, more calmly, he approached until he was touching me; looking at me seriously he said, "What were you shouting about?" I didn't know what to answer. One of the boys said, "We were talking about soccer; these two—all they do is argue whether Bologna or Genoa is better." Nicola turned quickly, making a fist as if he wished to hit the boy, then turned back to me. "Is it true that you were only talking about soccer? Swear to me," he said. He was red in the face, his eyes shiny with determination and rage. "I swear," I said. Nicola seemed to calm down. He took me by the arm. "Come on," he said. I followed him. We headed out of town, walking quickly in the direction of the road that led to the monastery. The monastery stood at a turning in a path that, leaving the road, climbed a low hill just outside the city. From up there you could see the river and a bridge, streets and squares, buildings and factories with their chimneys, and to the south, a little beyond the last houses, the place where I was born. It was like a city in miniature, with structures made of wood, and, following our imagination, we shifted at our pleasure houses, squares, streets. This was a game that, in the past, Paolo, Mario, Lucia, and I had spent entire afternoons playing. At the memory of it I was overcome with emotion, and I wished that someone would appear, that Nicola would make some move, anything. We walked rapidly toward the monastery. The woods behind it, which until late autumn flamed with red leaves, were now gray. Not all the trees had lost their leaves, but it was as if, overhung by the green foliage of the ilexes, they were no longer alive. Nicola, on my left, slowed down and every so often squeezed my arm as if he wanted to talk. We reached the monastery, which was poor, whitewashed, with no monks' tombs, nothing; Nicola had never gone on the outings to Monte Luca, which we could see in the distance, nor was he one who might propose going to an abbey or a church to pray. I looked at him, to encourage him to speak, but his face was covered by a woolen scarf, and I couldn't see it. Below us the city was cold, lifeless, with its avenues of bare trees, a few inhabitants hurrying along the streets. My fear that Nicola had heard his sister's name sharpened. I took his hand and nodded toward the way home, but he abruptly held me back. "You swore that you were talking about soccer and I believe you. We're too good friends for me to doubt you," he said. "But it seemed to me, when I was a few steps away, behind the kiosk, that I heard my sister's name. About my sister there is nothing to insinuate—she's not a whore, like a lot of their mothers and sisters." He kicked the ground violently, then shouted, "If my father finds out that someone in the city is making up some story about her, he'll strangle him." The cold that had descended on the hill suddenly penetrated me. Nicola must not know anything about Anna's relations with Luigi. I imagined the desperation of him and his father when, from a possible hint or an allusion by some malicious person, they learned of Anna's unbelievable love affair. That world, in which each of us could be caught and torn, and separated from others, was no longer habitable. I couldn't answer Nicola. I could no longer lie, nor did I know what to say. I tried to speak, but the words that came to me were shocking or brutal. I would have liked to embrace him, console him, convince him. I trembled, felt my throat constrict as if a hand were suffocating me. I started running, hurtling down the hill. When I stopped I was a few steps from the bridge that led to the city. I turned back: I couldn't see Nicola, he must still be at the monastery.

For the whole week I didn't see him. I went to the places where he usually was, but in vain. I even went to the carpenter's shop where he worked with his father, but the door was closed, and through the opaque, dirty windows you couldn't see inside.

A few days later, a Saturday, I was talking with the same boys who bought the adventure magazines, behind the kiosk, in the same sun-warmed corner. Suddenly I saw coming toward us, along the broad sidewalk that ringed the square, Nicola and his father. They were dressed up, in new coats and hats. They walked with firm, heavy steps, serious and proud, as if they were soldiers. They looked straight ahead without observing anyone. As they advanced they dug a furrow of grief in the paving stones of the street, in my thoughts, in those of the entire city. Everyone must in fact have felt what I did. Impulsively I came past the kiosk and approached the sidewalk. Nicola brushed past me without turning. Later I found out that they were going to

Luigi's to get Anna's letters. She was sent to live in another city with a sister of her father. For long days she stayed shut in the house. Nicola was no longer seen on the soccer field or at the kiosk. The rare times I met him, where I never expected to, he lowered his head, gave a hint of a smile between sad and affectionate, and fled, running. That smile disturbed me: it meant clearly that it was now impossible for us to stay friends.

I had just one cousin, Elio, who was the son of a wealthy brother of my father, and lived in a nearby city, the one I liked best of all the cities I had seen so far. Every year Elio and I spent a few weeks together at the house of our paternal grandmother, who lived in the country. I felt uneasy with Elio, who constantly imposed on me his father's wealth. It was in fact my uncle who brought us in his car to grandmother's and came to pick us up. Elio, after his father had already reproached me, said that I didn't know how to get in a car, that I banged the doors, that I got the upholstery dirty with my muddy shoes. To ensure that I would savor the difference between us, he wore blue oxford shirts and brown ties, all different; he told me about books his parents had given him and ones he had bought himself. This subtle arrogance brought me back to the time, not so long before, when my mother and grandmother had had to resort to innumerable expedients in order to put together the outfit I needed for the school play; and those wounds returned vividly, signaling a real difference that seemed to me unbridgeable. We were the same age, but even in front of grandmother Elio ordered me around as if I were a young servant; if someone had to go to the cellar to get wine, it was always me, and he would even refuse to go with me. He took offense because of the kindness that my natural, courteous manners inspired in the landowners and farmers in the villas and farmhouses near grandmother's; and tried to get revenge on me and humiliate me in every way. I wanted to obey him, support-ing him in his impossible whims, repressing my impulses to rebel. The more grandmother defended me and rebuked him for his aggressive behavior, the more Elio hated me; often he couldn't control himself and treacher-ously pummeled me.

He wanted to go on a long bike ride with me and a friend of ours, the son of a farmer who lived close by. The route was alluring; we would go several kilometers to the south, cross the countryside in the direction of the city where Elio lived, stop in two towns with extensive ruins of ancient castles, pass by a Spanish fort that was almost intact, and return to grandmother's house—a kind of broad circle drawn in the vast countryside. We left in early afternoon. A descent led to the center of the first town. Elio was in the lead, speeding along. Halfway down the slope, he shouted to us to stop because he had broken the spoke of a wheel. He bent forward to better observe the damage, straightened up in the saddle and made a sign to keep going because everything was fine, but then, a few meters farther on, he stopped, braking suddenly, which caused him to skid across the road. I was just behind. If I had tried to go around him on the left—on the right it was impossible because we were at the edge of the fields—our friend, who was following me fast and close, would have crashed into me. I braked, but couldn't stop in as short a distance as I hoped. I landed on top of him. The sharp tip of the fender of my heavy German bicycle hit him in the rear, tearing his pants and his underpants, and cutting him. When, touching the spot, he felt blood, he threw the bicycle into the middle of the road and tried to attack me. He cried that I had done it on purpose, that I was a tramp, a beggar, a liar, a coward. Then he ran to a pile of rocks next to the road, grabbed a big one, and hurled it at me, hitting my leg. Red in the face, swollen with rage, he sat by the side of the road. When he calmed down, he said that he couldn't go through the two towns and the other places with that rip in his pants, and when we got home grandmother, on seeing it, would reprimand him and send him back to his father; no one must find out. Our companion knew a family that lived in the first town we would come to; there a woman, a friend of his, would sew up the pants. We entered the town on foot, holding our bicycles by the handlebars, and my cousin pressing his left buttock with his hand; on the back of his knee there were bloodstains. We found the house of our companion's friends, and an old woman, with an ironic smile, sewed up the pants as best she could, every so often making some appreciative remark about Elio's plumpness. The bad job and the old woman's jokes rekindled my cousin's rage and he came out of the house without even thanking her. The whole way back Elio inveighed not only against me but against our friend, threatening to get back at us when we least expected it. The fury that continuously overwhelmed him, the stone he had thrown at me during the trip depressed both me and the other boy, revealing a malice that we hadn't suspected. When we reached grandmother's house it was very late. Grandmother scolded us and we justified ourselves by the length of the trip. Elio spoke without ever turning around, and she didn't notice anything. The next morning my cousin put on another pair of pants. He smiled, and his resentments seemed to have vanished utterly. Around midday, as I was waiting for lunch, I went to sit on the walk that surrounded the house, on the side that was out of the sun. Suddenly grandmother shouted at me to get up; I turned, moving slightly; a brick fell from above, landing just a step away. I heard grandmother slap Elio, who, shouting, confessed that he had wanted to kill me to get revenge for the tear I had made in his pants and the wound in his bottom. He had taken a brick from a pile near the chicken coop, waited till I sat down in the shade, and tried to hit me. Grandmother had arrived in time to divert the blow. Offended, she sent Elio away; after a few days I, too, went home.

The summer before my high-school exams, my mother, her sister Rosalba, my cousin Vera, and I went to spend July and August in the country at a place called Le Torri. It was a small village, some twenty kilometers out of the city in the direction of the sea. A large villa with two towers, which gave the place its name, loomed over a collection of smaller villas and a dozen or so farmhouses, one attached to the other, and, in the middle, Pietro's shop—a large space where he sold everything, and two smaller rooms, where in winter the young people of Le Torri and the neighboring towns, La Foce and San Leonardo, came to play cards and dance. A little apart from the other buildings was the church. The village stretched along one side of the road, almost hidden by the big villa if you were coming from the city. On the other side, opposite Pietro's shop, there was only a threshing floor, ten times the size of those found beside the farmhouses. In the past, when the whole village was the property of the Villa delle Torri, the farmers threshed their grain there, husked the corn, boxed or packed other products. Now that the land had been divided, by numerous sales, among many owners, the threshing floor was no longer of any use to anyone. There remained no storehouse, no roof to shelter the animals. It had become a sort of village square, where from late spring to autumn the young men and girls of Le Torri and from the surrounding area, both the wealthy and the farmers, gathered in the evenings. On the feast day of the village's patron saint a festival was held there, with strings of lights, dancing, and demijohns of sweet white wine that boys and girls offered to all.

My mother and aunt had rented a small house near the church. The day we arrived at Le Torri I discovered a field of sunflowers that came up to the hedge around our house and extended almost as far as the big threshing floor. I was amazed by its expanse. From the threshing floor the land descended steeply, in narrow terraces buttressed by rough stone walls, down to a cool green space where stands of oaks and hazelnuts and a few pines were visible, and, in the distance, you could see a river flowing. It was afternoon, late. The bricks of the threshing floor were pale pink and the sun had scattered a warm dust over them. In the village no one was around. That evening, after dinner, Vera and I went to the threshing floor and found some twenty people gathered in three groups, talking and walking. Soon we met boys and girls a few years older than us who invited us to their houses. My mother and aunt, too, found friends among women their age. Often a young man played a violin, and couples formed and danced, including the country dances called out by an old farmer with thick white hair who, to see the dancers better, climbed up on a wall of the threshing floor.

The house we lived in was old, and to keep it clean my mother and aunt were helped by Gino, a young man of twenty, of medium build, who was the son of a farmer. From ten to twelve, Gino swept the rooms, polished the brick floors, sorted the clothes for the laundry. He had immediately made friends with Vera and me: he brought us fruit and flowers and, one morning, a small blackbird that every so often let out a soft whistle, and followed people around. I saw Gino only in those two hours of the morning; one day I asked if I could go out with him in the afternoon, too, but he lowered his eyes and his lips formed an equivocal smile. There was no point in looking for him in the countryside, on the farm that his father worked, in the other fields along the river. I dragged Vera along on explorations of our surroundings, and she complained because it wasn't easy for her to get other people to like her and she was almost always left alone in the house. She seemed attracted to Gino while he was working, but he didn't so much as glance at her.

When I least expected it, one afternoon after cleaning the rooms Gino took me to the sunflower field. Sky and earth were at the height of a heavy, enervating heat. Passing the first few scattered plants, we penetrated farther in, where they grew more thickly, taller than us, their huge flowers all turned in one direction. Fierce hornets left the flowers to attack us, as they would have attacked any intruder whose footsteps made a stalk or leaf vibrate. Gino said that there was no danger because the hornets knew him, but that I should be careful and stay close to him: he told me about snakes and large mice the hornets had killed. The sunflowers also seemed to be living, insidious beings who, for mysterious reasons, offered the hornets shelter and rich, exciting nourishment. I advanced, hunched and anxious, behind Gino, who, alert, kept off the hornets that came too close to his face with a branch of bloodtwig torn from a low hedge. I stayed in the shelter of his raised arm and his broad shoulders. Strangely, at times the sunflowers, too, turned threatening toward us; bent by the weight of their seed-packed flowers and their fleshy leaves, or by the force of the sun, they would suddenly straighten, to sink again among the neighboring stalks; then, without warning, they would strike me sharply in the back. When we reached the middle of the field we found a small open space: the sunflowers thinned out, becoming dense again farther on. Gino sat on the bare earth and I imitated him. For a while he said nothing, then he told me that if I wanted to see him in the afternoons I would find him here, but I should never let Vera come, nor tell her that he had brought me to the sunflower field. The next morning Gino said to me as he was leaving, "Today we'll meet there." In the afternoon, when Vera and my mother and aunt went off to rest, I left the house and, crouching, almost on all fours, fearful but driven by a tormenting attraction, entered the sunflower field. Gino was waiting for me. He had a pruning knife sharpened like a blade and a dark cloth sack. He pulled out a guinea pig, killed it with the pruning knife by cutting its belly, then, after giving it a lengthy examination, flung it far away from us. He told me that the hornets liked the flesh. Meanwhile the sunflowers were still; the hornets slept on the seeds gathered inside the yellow flowers. Time passed. Then Gino made me a sign to get up. He went to one of the biggest sunflowers, tore out a handful of seeds, and offered them to me. He said, "Eat them, they're better than pumpkin seeds." Eluding Vera, I returned to the clearing many times. I always found Gino sitting on the ground. One day he told me that he was a friend of the hornets and the sunflowers and always brought them some little beast to eat that he had killed with the pruning knife. Often he took from his bag small hedgehogs that he hunted in the fields. Then he would become silent, motionless, staring straight ahead, like the sentinel of that little fort whose walls were made up of yellow flowers, now bent and sleeping, now stretched toward the sun. He always gave me some seeds that he plucked from one of the tallest and biggest sunflowers.

One afternoon Gino asked me if I had ever been with a woman. I said no. "Not even with Vera?" he said in astonishment. "No," I said. "It's not possible," Gino said. "She's always near at hand. She's a pretty girl, ready to make love. I've seen her sex. She always sits on the stairs with her legs spread. She has a pink sex, it looks like a clean wound. Sometimes I feel like bringing her here, then sticking the tip of the pruning knife into her, ripping her apart like a guinea pig, and leaving her to the hornets. If you come back next year I'll take care of it." I made a gesture of revulsion. Sensations that had hit me many times without ever becoming precise now came clearly into my mind. I, too, had seen Vera's sex, but at the first word from her mother everything vanished into the naturalness of daily life. Sometimes in the garden, when there weren't enough chairs, Vera said to me, "Sit on my lap," and smoothed her skirt. My aunt intervened: "It's true you're cousins, but such invitations aren't proper. Even he is a man." And the thoughts took another direction. Now Gino insisted: "You city people are way behind us. Here the young men and even boys lie in wait for hours and hours to surprise a couple making love on the edge of a wood or in a ditch, then they make the girls do the same with them. They assault girls and even married women who are alone in the fields or just a little apart from their group, at harvest time, when the women don't even know who's lying on top of them."

A few days later, Vera wasn't sleepy after lunch and delayed going to her room. She was sitting outside in a chair, with her legs crossed. Next to her, I remembered Gino's words: I felt a desire to caress her head and neck and, on the other hand, I was thinking how to get free and run to the sunflower field, where Gino was waiting for me. My aunt looked out the window and said, "Vera, if you're not sleepy, at least study a little. In all these days, I haven't seen you pick up a book." Vera huddled in the chair, but her mother and also mine insisted: "Vera, come, be good. If you aren't going to study we have a little job for you." In a soft voice Vera said to me, turning slowly, "Wait for me." She went into the house. As soon as I saw her talking to the women on the little balcony above the door, I got up and ran toward the sunflower field. After a few steps I heard Vera running and calling me. I threw myself headlong among the stalks, careful not to bump them, not to give my cousin any sign of where I was. Then I crept on hands and knees until I reached Gino, who was standing up, waiting for me. He didn't have the pruning knife. The sunflowers were all straight on their stalks, intently feeding on the blinding, abundant light of the sun. I was afraid that Vera had discovered us and wanted to know what we did when we were alone. Then that she would fall prey to Gino, that they had met and made a plan. In the field not a sound could be heard, but I didn't have the courage to keep from telling Gino that Vera was looking for me. At that point, Gino changed direction; he walked to the side away from the villa and we came out of the sunflower field; fenced by barbed wire, it bordered on a large field of clover. Gino found an opening in the barbed wire and led me toward the threshing floor. We crossed it and rushed down the grassy slope, grabbing onto the branches of the hazelnut trees. We reached the river, followed it for a hundred meters, crossed it on stepping-stones, and entered the thicket of oaks and hazelnuts visible from the threshing floor. Farther on, behind a compact row of trees, there was a small hut, made of broom, whose roof sloped down almost to the ground. At most two people could enter. Outside the door, also of broom, were three young men, not even twenty: two sitting on the lush grass, one standing next to the hut. The door opened and another boy came out, perhaps my age. I saw a young girl lying on a straw pallet with her dress pulled up above her belly. My sight dimmed for an instant: I was afraid it was Vera. But the young man who was standing made a sign to Gino, who told him to go in. My fears evaporated and I was seized by a desirous excitement. One after another the young men went into the hut and came back out, always with Gino's consent. They sat silently off on their own. Gino went in, too. I heard the girl cry, "No, no." Gino came out, his face tense and threatening. He took me by the arm and pushed me inside the hut. The girl barely looked at me and began shouting again, "Go away, I don't want to, it's not like with the others." She was a very young girl, with curly black hair. She pulled her blue dress up over her face, uncovering her body below her bare chest: she was slender and shapely and olive-skinned. Her muffled cries reached me through the material of the dress. "Not you, not you—go away." Then she turned over onto her stomach and began to cry. Gino entered in a fury, knelt down beside her, put his hand between her thighs and tried force, but he couldn't make her turn. The girl tensed her body, shook her head, shouted. "Go with his cousin, take them all there," she said. Gino hit her in the head with his fist. "The sons of the rich are just like us, stupid." Gino took me by the arm and dragged me out of the hut. "Do you make her go with everyone?" I asked. "Not just her," Gino said. I looked up toward the threshing floor: it seemed so high above me, an inaccessible mountain. I felt drained. On the image of that naked, screaming, beaten girl, who seemed crazed, were superimposed those of Rosa, Vera, my mother, my aunt. The love I had felt for Rosa, Vera's sex, what I had seen in the hut whirled in my mind. Gino looked at me in surprise. He took me by the shoulders, shook me. "If you say a word of what you've seen I'll break all your teeth," he said. Grabbing my arm he forced me to climb, faster and faster. He stopped and said, "One day or other I'll find you a girl, so you'll get to know them and you won't ever forget." I ran home and told my mother what I had seen. I urged her to tell my aunt to keep a close watch on Vera and not to let her go out alone.

I didn't go to the sunflower field for several days and didn't see Gino; nor did he come in the mornings to help my mother and aunt. But one afternoon, hurrying to Pietro's shop to buy some soap, I saw that Gino was standing in the doorway as if he'd been expecting me. He was staring at two girls who were walking on the threshing floor, and who until then had not been seen in Le Torri. They were dark-haired, sturdy. They looked at us, then one of them, in a loose deep-blue dress with a tie around the waist that showed off the fullness of her hips, broke off from the other, smoothed her hair, and, holding her skirt, walked toward us. We hadn't left the shop doorway. She turned back and walked across the threshing floor, treading with the heels and toes of her shoes the dust that had accumulated on the wide bricks. Her legs were bare, and strong; the blue skirt made them seem even more bare. After walking around the other girl, she crouched on her heels, touched the brick dust with her fingers, gathered it into a little pile, and stuck her hands in it, looked at her hands, and rubbed them on her legs. She got up and, still treading on the bricks with the heels and toes of her shoes, she went back to the other girl and started talking to her in an undertone. I hadn't missed a detail of Gino's expression as he stared at the girl's movements, his body relaxed. I was so absorbed in watching Gino that I no longer remembered anything about what I had seen in the hut. As if nothing had happened in the days before he said to me, "That girl should spend some time with me, in the hut." He added, "Come down to the sunflower field." Just then the two girls gestured to us. We approached. The one in the blue dress was called Alba, the other Marina. They were the daughter and niece of a wealthy merchant from a city in the north who a few months earlier had bought a villa in the neighborhood. Alba asked if in Le Torri there were girls and boys to go around with, walk in the fields, if it was possible to dance. Gino answered that if she came to the threshing floor in the evening she would find all the inhabitants of Le Torri and the neighboring villages. Marina asked the names of the villas that we could see from there, the name of the river, and if beyond the thicket of oaks and hazelnuts, an area that was out of sight, the fields began again. When dinnertime approached, Alba and Marina went off on their bicycles, which they had left leaning against a wall of the threshing floor. I noticed that Gino and Alba had stood very close together as they talked and that at times the girl stared at the young man with her face thrust forward.

That same evening Alba and Marina returned to Le Torri and met people. Alba asked to dance and Gino rushed to call Tommaso, the musician, who hadn't yet arrived. Gino, who was wearing a pair of brown pants and a white shirt, immediately started dancing with Alba. If she danced with someone else, he followed her with his gaze, waiting patiently for his turn to come again. When, past midnight, we went home, Gino told Alba that in the next few days he would show her a stretch of the river with a small open space where you could swim and a grove of hazelnut trees beyond the thicket of oaks. I thought that Gino wanted to set a trap for Alba, but I was afraid to warn her, because a strange timidity seized me at the idea of talking to her alone.

Alba and Marina never came to Le Torri during the afternoon, but, rested and unadorned, they were always the first to arrive in the evening. It seemed to me that Alba encouraged Gino to stay close to her in such a way that the others, separating into couples, would leave the two of them apart. Even when they danced they would move to where there was more space, often skirting the walls of the big threshing floor.

Gino still didn't show up at our house; but in the afternoons he always retreated to the sunflower field. If I made
my way amid the stalks I'd find him lying on the ground
with his arms crossed under his head, and almost always
quiet. He no longer brought small beasts for the hornets
and the sunflowers, or even the pruning knife. It seemed
to me that he had a hard time speaking, as if he were ham-
pered by a thought that I couldn't understand. One day in
early August, not finding him among the sunflowers, I
turned back and, passing through the garden, came to the
threshing floor. It was deserted. I sat on the wall, on the
cliff side. Suddenly I saw two specks moving down beyond
the oaks and the hazelnuts. They disappeared and then
reappeared on this side of the trees. Gradually, as they got
closer, I recognized Gino and Alba. Now they were walking a little apart. Gino began the ascent first. He held out
his hand to Alba, but at that gesture she stopped, choosing to help herself, and held on to a tuft of grass. When
they were near the road they stopped. They stood for some
minutes looking at each other; Gino gestured to her to
come closer, she shook her head; then the young man
jumped up on the road and rushed off toward his house.
Alba, walking lazily, went to get her bicycle, which, hidden
behind the wall of the threshing floor, I hadn't noticed.

The next day I found Gino in the sunflower field. He
was kneeling on the ground, digging a hole in the earth
with the pruning knife. His movements were so furious
that it seemed he was hurrying to bury the body of some
animal that was bothering him, but I couldn't see anything
around. As soon as he saw me he got up. "Come on," he
said and headed toward the provincial road. A few yards
ahead of us, among the last sunflowers, we noticed a big

snake that was to cross our path. Gino stopped, with one hand held me behind him, stroked his hair, then raised the pruning knife to the height of the sunflowers and hurled it at the snake, hitting it above the head; the snake writhed, but the pruning knife held it firm against the ground. Gino grabbed the pruning knife again and with a sharp blow cut off the snake's head. He picked up the body and wrung it, so that a reddish liquid came oozing out. Holding the snake by the tail, he crossed the last bit of the field. I followed him. Unexpectedly, we saw Alba and Marina on the threshing floor, with two young men we didn't know. Gino whispered to me, "I'd do her in just like that snake. She wouldn't even lie down beside me." Alba was walking on the pink dust of the bricks with the heels and the toes of her shoes, just as she had the day we met her. Gino went up to her and threw the snake at her feet. Alba, not at all surprised, turned the snake over and over with the tip of one shoe, then bent down to touch it. She rolled the reptile until it was covered with dust, taking on its color. Alba stood up, smiled at Gino, and asked him, "Where did you kill it? I have a friend who wraps live snakes around her arms. I'm not afraid of them, either. Let's go find another one." Gino turned around and headed toward the sunflower field. Alba followed without saying goodbye. I looked at Gino and Alba disappearing among the fat yellow flowers, still gorging on their meal of sunlight. I couldn't understand why Alba, her friend, and the two young men had been on the sunny threshing floor at that unusual hour, and why Gino had, with such confidence, in front of everyone, thrown the snake at her feet, after what he had said to me before. And why she had invited him to go with her to find another snake in the sunflower field, where Gino wouldn't bring anyone. I crossed the street, went into the garden, and ran to the sunflower field. I crawled among the plants to reach the space where Gino usually was, but no one was there. The sun, quickly retreating, left the air cleaner and lighter, and the big flowers were slowly beginning to bend over their stalks. I found myself in another part of the field, where the clover began. Crossing those fields I came to a villa with a farmhouse next to it. On the steps of the house sat Gino, Alba, and two farm boys. Gino was playing with the pruning knife, pointing at places in the countryside. After a while he jumped to his feet and Alba, to pull herself up, held out her hands to him. I slowly backed away. For several days after that afternoon I couldn't bring myself to see either Gino or Alba. I was overcome by an acute, mysterious fear and often had to take refuge in the house, staying close to Vera, until the anxiety vanished, leaving me in a room that did not belong to any house, that was not in any place on earth.

On the evening of August 10th in Le Torri, inhabitants and vacationers celebrated San Lorenzo. The threshing floor was decorated with oak boughs, with ferns and paper lanterns. We were all there that night. After several dances, a dark-haired girl arrived, named Sara, who, as I later found out, was the daughter of well-off farmers in the area. She had been studying in a distant city, and just that year had finished teacher-training school. After the exams she had spent a month at the seaside with a maternal aunt and for that reason had arrived at Le Torri later than in previous years. Everyone congratulated her and made a toast to her. Sara sat next to Gino and danced with him often.

They had known each other since childhood and seemed to be close friends. Alba didn't dance when Gino did. She sat apart. Suddenly she got up, started walking on her toes and heels, and approached Gino decisively. It seemed to me that she wanted to talk to him, that she wanted to separate him from Sara. Just then, some youths from a nearby village arrived and asked if they could join the celebration. They were very self-assured and kept asking Alba and Sara to dance. Around midnight a farmer brought a large yellow pumpkin into the middle of the threshing floor. "Come on, let's make a lantern," he said. He had a candle. "Give me a hand," he said. Tommaso stopped playing and the dancing couples separated, forming a circle around the pumpkin and the farmer. The farmer couldn't cut the top off the pumpkin with his knife—it was too hard and big. So Gino went to get his pruning knife and, slicing sharply all around, took it off. Alba and Gino got on their knees and, plunging their hands into the yellow pulp, struggled to tear out the ribs and seeds. "We need some help," said Alba. One of the young men from the neighboring village who had been dancing with her knelt down and thrust a strong hand inside the pumpkin. From the laughter, from certain abrupt movements, you could tell that his fingers were meeting Gino's and Alba's. Gino got tired and sat on the floor with his head resting on his knees. Alba and the other man kept on, joking and laughing. Even when the pumpkin was empty, they stayed there, smoothing the inside with their hands. Maybe they were holding hands, because Alba cried out and began laughing. Gino, who had again come close to her, brusquely pushed the young man aside. He leaned over and with the pruning knife cut mouth and eyes in the pumpkin. The farmer who had brought it to the threshing floor lit the candle, placed it inside the pumpkin, and put back the top, which he had been holding in his hand. The pumpkin illuminated the center of the threshing floor, and Tommaso began to play a dance tune. The threshing floor filled with couples, even the old farmers, all dancing around the pumpkin. Gino asked Alba to dance, but she said she was going to dance with the young man who had helped her clean out the pumpkin. Gino took her by the arm, but with a hostile gesture she freed herself and went toward the other young man, who was waiting for her. The candle inside the pumpkin went out. A cry was heard and something metal hit the floor. Alba touched her shoulder and said, "There's blood." Then she cried, "Gino did it." The dancers gathered around her. The doctor was called, and said that the wound didn't seem serious but told Alba to come to his office. A farmer picked up Gino's pruning knife: it was scarcely bloodied. Alba told the others to go on dancing; she would go alone with the doctor, who would give her some stitches. A dozen young men, including the one who had danced with her and his friends from the neighboring village, said they were going to look for Gino, catch him and take him to the police. They began talking about where he might be hiding. Certainly Gino had struck Alba out of jealousy, because she refused to dance with him. Meanwhile the hunt for the attacker grew rowdier and more agitated. Several young men and girls came to our house to rest, and my mother and aunt gave them drinks. The moon illuminated the houses, the garden, the roads, and the threshing floor. Someone had relit the candle inside the pumpkin. I stood off to the side, frightened by the threats people were shouting, by the sticks some were brandishing. I had seen how Gino behaved with that poor girl down in the hut, but what those people, as their excitement increased, were preparing for him would be more terrifying. It wasn't possible to live among other people if all of a sudden they could attack one another with such ferocity. The sunflowers absorbed less moonlight than the house, the street, the meadows, the other plants and trees. I alone knew Gino's hiding place, but I said nothing, even if I condemned him, if I felt revulsion, even if I was sure that for a long time the memory of Alba's wounding would disturb my days.

A week later, my mother, my aunt, my cousin, and I left Le Torri. Soon my school days would be starting up again, my last, and the most intense, though I was well prepared. The return to the city calmed me, put my feelings in order, distanced into an infinite past the events I had just witnessed. Death, the breakdown of affections, love, traps, hatred, revenge no longer seemed to me indispensable elements of people's lives. The coin purse belonging to the young Roman found when I was at the excavations with my grandfather, then living, came to my mind, like a propitious warning, whenever I felt sorrow or joy.

Even my love for Rosa and its dissipation, Anna's love for Luigi, Nicola's desperation, the obscure struggle between Gino and Alba had not dug a deep, incurable wound within me. Day by day my old feelings abated, and, completely absorbed in studying, I was even able to form a judgment about them. I had heard my mother and grandmother say that women age before men, and considering that Rosa was a year older than me I found it right that she was engaged. Only when I was much older would

I marry, because I was going to become a doctor first. I thought with amusement and irony of my cousin's actions, of his violence, and with pride of my mother, who had triumphed over all the spiteful gossip that had piled up around her. Calm, and filled with the desire to succeed, I prepared for my exams. I had to take them in the capital city of the region, because the school I went to was not a public school. Ten days before the exams, my mother and I went to that city, as the guests of a family who were old friends of ours, from the time when grandfather and grandmother had the hotel. They lived in a beautiful house at the end of a street, near one of the oldest city gates, and the family was composed of the father, Antonio, the mother, Sandra, the son, Mauro, and the daughter, Lidia, and her husband, Federico. Many years before, Sandra had been the head of a fashion house. She made bimonthly visits to my city and presented her designs in the meeting room of the hotel. Sometimes the shows lasted an entire week. Sandra became a friend of my grandmother and, especially, my grandfather, and after several stays they refused to let her pay not only for the use of the room but even for food and lodging. Sandra recalled my grandfather with great fondness, and she would laugh heartily as she recounted small incidents of his life. She told me that one night, during a very cold winter, she was talking with my grandparents in the large, well-heated kitchen of the hotel, when, not long before they went to bed, a tenor arrived, who was to sing two days later in *Carmen*. The tenor hadn't eaten during his journey, and was cold and tired. He warmed himself at the hearth, where a big oak log was still burning, then he asked for some hot broth. Grandfather had nothing freshly made, because every night, after the kitchen was cleaned, he gave the day's leftovers to the poor. He decided to prepare the broth with a good beef concentrate. He took out a new jar and soon the broth was ready; but the concentrate was spoiled. During the night the guest had a violent stomach ache and bouts of vomiting and diarrhea, and in the morning he had almost lost his voice. He sang but he was booed. The audience was astonished, because the tenor was well known in the city, and had sung there other times, and in *Carmen*, with great success. No one could have imagined that grandfather was the involuntary cause of that disaster, not even the tenor, who blamed the cold.

Sandra gave my mother and me a warm welcome and prepared for us a large room whose walls were covered in blue wallpaper with golden flowers. The bedspread and the carpet were blue, too. She made a fuss over me. Antonio regarded me with good nature and urged me to study; Mauro was always joking and the day I arrived took me to see his big storerooms full of fabrics in bulk, and said that if I passed my exams he would give me a piece of material for a suit. The next day, Sunday, he took me, my mother, and his sister, Lidia, to the hippodrome to see the horse races. During those first days Federico appeared only at Sunday lunch. He was a robust, stocky man, with thin red hair and stubby hands, vulgar in his way of sitting, speaking, eating. A fruit wholesaler at the market, he had to be at his place of work every day at four in the morning. He had lunch out, and at night he ate dinner early and went immediately to bed. Lidia was a beautiful woman, younger than her husband, with dark hair and a voluptuous figure; she had sloping shoulders, round arms, and high small breasts. At home she wore short, sleeveless, low-cut dresses. Every afternoon we went out, she, my mother, and I, to the movies or to the shops in the city center. Lidia's clothes were very tight: her nipples were large for her young breasts and pressed against the fabric that covered them. When we were alone my mother said that if Lidia were her daughter she would never allow her to dress like that: her small swaying steps attracted the attention of men, and even boys turned to look at her. Lidia told us that she had been engaged many times, that men liked her a lot, that often at the movies someone would try to touch her breast or thighs; she never said anything to her husband and brother, who accompanied her, but used a long straight pin to keep off the hands that reached for her body—a game she found very entertaining. Even now that she wore a wedding ring men young and old stopped her on the street to make declarations of love. She complained about Federico: his life didn't suit her, too often he made her a prisoner of his work hours. Sunday was the only day Federico had free, but he often wanted to keep his wife in bed. She, on the other hand, would have liked to have a livelier, more carefree life.

My mother left after a few days, in order not to take advantage of our friends' hospitality. She would be returning shortly before the exams were over. So I was alone with Sandra and her family. The exams began; I was well prepared and didn't have any problems. Unfortunately, the exams would last a long time, because there were a lot of candidates and they came from the entire region. I left in the morning at nine and returned around midday. We had lunch at a round table. Antonio was silent, as if he were an unwelcome guest in the family, Sandra talked about everything and often indulged in memories of the days when she ran the fashion house and stayed at my grandfather's hotel. She declared that my grandfather was the nicest man she had ever met and made the most varied, abundant meals, so much so that she still kept some recipes. Mauro and Lidia, on the other hand, asked me about my exams; they wanted me to tell them how I had worked out the essay topics I had been assigned; Lidia, moving her lips as if she were tasting a sweet, blew me a kiss across the table.

One Sunday morning the house was transformed. Windows and doors were thrown open for more than two hours. Until then I had known only my room, with two brass beds and a chest of drawers, the sitting room where we ate, and the little garden that the kitchen window looked out on. That morning I saw Antonio and Sandra's room, with a large, light-colored wardrobe that went up to the ceiling and a high, unmade bed. Lidia and Federico's room was also open. Federico, who had just had a bath, was standing in front of the mirror tying a yellow-polka-dotted green tie. I saw a small sitting room, papered in red velvet. Lidia was in a chair leafing through a newspaper. She was wearing a long pale-purple sort of dressing gown with a wide lace border at the shoulders and neck that left part of her bosom visible. She had unpinned her hair and let it fall around her shoulders. She invited me to sit on another chair. When Federico came out of the bedroom, he embraced her, touching her shoulders and breast. She yielded to him, holding him with one arm, her head on his shoulder; meanwhile she stared at me and her look was expressionless and cold. Finally she closed her eyes and I left the room, embarrassed more by that look than by her outfit and the embrace with Federico. At lunch three courses were brought to the table, three different types of wine, dessert and fruit. Antonio and Mauro ate quickly, heads bent over their plates. When we came to dessert, Federico seemed to have appeased his hunger. He smiled in satisfaction, looked around as if surprised to see us sitting at the same table. He reached out his arm and stuck his hand into Lidia's cleavage. Sandra made a gesture of chasing off a fly and laughed, and the others laughed; when they were quiet Federico's laugh remained suspended in the room. I was burning with shame. I glanced at Lidia; she was smiling indulgently, and every so often she shook her head and her hair came down to her chin. Federico took a handful of cherries and some large plums from the fruit bowl, dried his hands on the tablecloth, then reached out his right hand, felt Lidia's stomach for a long time, and, turning to me, staring into my eyes, said, "You'd be glad to touch my wife's bosom, wouldn't you?" I was sitting next to him, on his left. I couldn't withstand his gaze. I had the impulse to get up, but Federico, with his thick pale hand, quickly grabbed my arm with an irresistible force and compelled me to stay in my seat. He took me by the chin and tilted my head back so that I was looking straight at him. "Surely the little gentleman can't be shocked," he said, becoming suddenly threatening. "I'm sure he's had plenty of thoughts about women, maybe even about Lidia. You'd like that, eh! What were you doing before in the sitting room if not looking at her tits?" Meanwhile, with his other hand he picked up his glass and drank. He stared at me, without letting go of my face, and said, "You're made like the rest of us, no? At your age I was an errand boy for a fruit seller in the city center. My friend and I would go down to the basement and we'd look up through a grate that opened onto the sidewalk at the thighs of the women passing by and at what they have between their thighs." I began to cry. "Leave him alone, Federico," said Sandra. "You can see they've brought him up in cotton wool, though his grandfather was no saint and he liked a bawdy story." "What do you mean, cotton wool," said Federico. "I'll take him to the market and unplug his ears. Boys today know a thing or two, and you can be sure that even he knows what's what. Look and see if his sheets are clean." I was still crying, with my head on the table. The most subtle workings of my consciousness were being shattered, I felt changed, dirty, incapable of showing my face to my classmates, or the professors. It seemed to me that the veils that shrouded the moves of Gino, of Alba, of everyone I had known had been suddenly stripped away—veils that not even Gino's pruning knife had managed to shred. My mind was fixed on my mother. The thought that that Sunday she might have been there, beside me, obliged to observe Federico caressing Lidia, to hear his words, made me blush even redder with shame, shame that was transformed into terror. Now as I wept I was trembling. "You can go to your room. With a nice nap it will all pass," said Sandra. "The little gentleman is also rude," said Mauro. "He's behaving as if he were in his own house. Before he gets up he has to have dessert and fruit. He'll leave the table when we do." With an angry push he made me raise my head. I could eat neither dessert nor fruit. Thrust upright, I sat still at the table, staring at the wall. Everyone was silent. Lidia finally brought the coffee, Federico drank it very hot, bent over his cup, drumming with his fingers on the table. I looked at him. His body had become heavy, his gaze clouded. The

minutes went by slowly. It seemed to me that he was staying there as long as possible to prolong my torment. At last
he got up and nodded to Lidia to follow him. "Let's go
back to bed," he said. He headed, unsteadily, toward his
room. He let Lidia go first, pushing her, one hand on her
rear. Before closing the door he turned toward the sitting
room, sought me out with his dull gaze, and, pointing a
finger at me, said, "Wouldn't you like to be where, in a little while, I'll be going." Sandra came over and patted me
on the head. "Men are like that," she said. Together with
Antonio she, too, left the table.

Finally I was able to take refuge in my room. I sat on a
chair and laid my head on the bed. It was the end of July,
the window had been open for a long time, and the room
was hot. Federico's last words had struck me like a fist. A
vague fear assailed me, then became precise, resolving
itself into the dread of seeing soon again the people who
were my hosts, especially Federico and Lidia. I had to stay
in that house for several more days, and that was the
thought that tormented me most. I would have liked to
write to mamma. I was afraid that, grateful for the long
hospitality I had received, she would not understand my
feelings and would side with Federico and the others.
Because of the heaviness of the meal and the heat of the
room I was at the limits of physical resistance. Gradually,
I fell asleep. I woke after two hours. The reasons for my
tears seemed more and more mysterious. The tense, disturbing atmosphere that had enveloped the sitting room
earlier had vanished. Federico's words now sounded like
market vulgarities, the complicity of the others a way of
amusing themselves. There was a knock at the door. It was

Sandra. "I want to introduce you to a person who knew your grandfather well and often stayed in his hotel." Everything had returned to the normal and familiar. Sandra led me into the red sitting room. A man of Federico's height, who vaguely resembled him, sat beside the little table. "This is my nephew Cesare, the actor, who's performed often in your city," she said proudly. The man shook my hand, lowering his head. When he raised it I saw that he was weeping. Addressing Sandra, he continued a conversation that must have begun some time earlier. "My name dragged through the papers in a huge, disgusting scandal. People won't believe that I was in the dark about everything. And how could she think she wouldn't be found out? She said she felt safe because she had also provided her services to important people. And I believe it. But when someone dies you can't close your eyes. An abortion, a hundred abortions—you know? I'm disgraced, and she, wretched woman, is in prison. I know how she is: without men, without comforts, without proper food, despised by everyone—she'll die." "It's a terrible calamity that's happened. But everything will pass. At least if there were divorce in this country," Sandra said. "It will also take some time to find work now," said Cesare. "Don't worry about money, we'll help you, you're the only relative we have, the one who kept up our reputation, who let the world know we existed. You remember that Lidia wanted to marry you?" said Sandra. She looked around as if she were pursuing an idea, a recourse. She caressed the man's head and said to him, "Meanwhile, tonight you'll stay and have dinner with us."

Outside it was getting dark. When Antonio came home—on Sunday he usually met friends at the café—we had dinner. Federico and Lidia weren't there; they had eaten in a restaurant in the center of town and gone to the movies. Antonio asked Cesare if everything the newspapers had published was true. So I learned the story of Lena. To increase their income, since Cesare was an actor who didn't earn much, Lena had opened a pensione. In need of guests, she had taken in pelota players and whoever showed up. She had two maids, Venetian like her, pretty and ready to go to bed with anyone. One of the girls got pregnant, and Lena had caused her to abort, with her own hands; she knew the business, having learned it from her mother, a midwife. After that first time, because it had been easy, Lena had continued to help the girls whom the two maids brought to the house, until one young woman died from loss of blood. I was sleepy, but every time I tried to leave Sandra and Cesare restrained me.

After midnight Lidia and Federico returned: they were hot but at the same time relaxed and rested as if after a long sleep. Federico smiled at me and Lidia patted my head. They talked for a long time about the disaster that had befallen Lena and Cesare. Then they all went to bed. I had to get up early in the morning for my exams, but I couldn't fall asleep. I thought with terror how my mother, a few days before we left our city, had told me that if Sandra couldn't have us we would go to the pensione of her niece Lena. To chase away that thought and try to sleep I got out my Latin grammar, but I knew all the rules by heart and had done the written exercises. I placed the book on the table in front of the window and sat down. I half-opened the blinds; the night was clear and cool. I got up and began to poke around the room. There was a small old wardrobe, which I opened; it was full of sheets and towels tied in bundles with pink and blue silk ribbons. I closed it and went over to the chest of drawers. It was tall, with four drawers, and had a green marble top, with a large mirror. I pulled the first drawer toward me. In a corner, one on top of the other, were some boxes; I opened one: it contained a candy box of solid silver with three sugared almonds in it, two white and one with a flower and four leaves painted on it. I took them and ate them, even the painted one. They were old and the almonds tasted rancid. I closed the candy box and then the other box. On the opposite side of the drawer there were satin bras, sanitary pads, underpants. I looked at them, one by one: blue, pink, black, white; they seemed very small to be Lidia's, but I was immediately sure that they were. Lidia often wore a gray dress of a light material through which her bosom and her long thighs were visible. I closed the drawer but in my rush left the edge of a pair of pink underpants sticking out. Frantically I opened the drawer and without refolding the underpants put them back in their place. Calming down I went to bed and fell asleep.

Two days later Lidia realized that I had been rummaging in the drawer, that I had looked at her underwear and eaten the almonds. Coming back from the Latin exams, I found Lidia and Sandra in my room. They had emptied the first drawer of the dresser and had placed the underwear and the boxes on the bed. Sandra attacked me. "It's a disgrace to behave like that in someone else's house, the house of friends. I'm telling your mother," she said. Lidia said nothing but she looked at me as if she meant to ask, "What else have you done behind our backs, that we haven't yet discovered?" She said, "Mamma, that's enough. The underwear is clean. Nothing is missing. What do you care about three sugared almonds that have gone bad by now." "It's not for three sugared almonds, which are worthless. It's for what they represented," said Sandra. "And what did they represent by now, after all these years?" said Lidia. "A souvenir of your marriage. Don't you know that it's bad luck to lose the wedding almonds?" Sandra said. "And what a fine marriage, too," said Lidia. "What? Aren't you happy? You found a man who kisses the ground you walk on, who thinks only of you, of work, of home. Who did you want to marry? Someone with an education? A scoundrel, like this little gentleman here is going to be?" said Sandra. Her face was distraught. "Mamma, now you're exaggerating. For three almonds. He didn't steal anything. He didn't even open all the boxes," Lidia said. "Rummaging around, sniffing your underwear? The candies—that's already a kind of sacrilege. You'll see, some disaster's going to happen to us now, after Lena's," said Sandra. "That disaster is ours, and it's not his fault," said Lidia. "Lena's in prison and she has our name," said Sandra, and she began putting back the underwear, smoothing it with her hand. Suddenly she left and Lidia continued the job. I was standing beside the window, silent, sunk in shame. The less valuable I considered the three candies, the more irreparable seemed to me the offense I had committed against the people who were my hosts and whom I had never given a thought to in that terrible moment. I wished to apologize, but I felt that if I uttered even a word I would cry. When she finished Lidia came over and took my face in her hands. "It's nothing. Don't be upset. You know how old people are. They're superstitious. I don't believe in anything, I never even go to church. I promise you, my mother won't make any more dramatic scenes and she won't say anything to the men. Anyway, there's not much to tell," she said. I felt the weight of her body pressing against my chest. She laughed. "Those damn almonds must have been pretty bad," she said, and I understood that she would have liked me to say something, to break the tension. She caressed me and left the room. I heard the house door open and close: it was Antonio and Mauro. After a while Lidia came to call me to lunch. I hadn't the courage to show up in the sitting room, but Lidia put a hand on my back and pushed me lightly. "Go on, no one will know anything. It's foolishness that will be forgotten right away: even my mother will be quiet," she said. The meal unfolded as usual in almost total silence. Sandra looked at me grimly. Lidia, on the other hand, urged me to eat, to better withstand the heat and the fatigue of the exams.

In the afternoon I went back to school for the exams in history and geography. Afterward I lingered on the streets and avenues. I was afraid of meeting Federico: it seemed to me impossible that Sandra's mean words would have no consequence. Then I hurried, in order to arrive as quickly as possible before my judges. I thought, "Consider everything, calmly, before condemning me," but I was aware that I would be unable to say those words. Federico and the others were waiting for dinner. Antonio and Lidia were already seated. Federico looked at me, with a serious expression. After the soup they began, as though they had agreed beforehand, to talk about Cesare and Lena. Sandra asked if it wouldn't be right to have Cesare stay in their house as soon as I left; he was alone, with the pensione closed, and no servant, and perhaps also with no money, because, at least at the moment, he wasn't a member of any theater company. Antonio and Mauro said they would have to discuss it carefully because Cesare was the only relative they had. The one who eagerly supported Sandra's proposal was Lidia. She said that it was really a duty to welcome Cesare and surround him with the affection that he surely needed now that Lena was in prison. But Federico was violently opposed. "It serves Cesare right. He shouldn't have married that woman who seems like the madam of a brothel. Everybody likes his pleasure, but then you have to pay for it," he said. Lidia said to him that the owners of the house were Antonio and Sandra, who would do what they wanted. "You always want a man underfoot. That's what you want," said Federico, banging his fist on the table. "If Cesare sets foot in this house I'm leaving," he added. Dinner was over and I got up, but Federico stopped me with a look. "As for you, you little rat, try going through my wife's underwear again—I'll spank you like a spoiled child and throw you out of the house," he cried. Lidia glanced at her mother in surprise; Sandra coldly half-closed her eyes in a sign of assent. Lidia began to cry. "Stop it, your tears are not convincing. Between us, I'm the one who will make the decisions," said Federico. Lidia got up and ran to her room. Turning to Sandra, Federico, calm but firm, said, "Let's not say anything more about Cesare and the rest." When everyone had got up from the table, I went into the garden. I felt fairly calm. In two days I would finish my exams and return home. It was very hot. Two tall Japanese medlars shielded the garden from the moon. I sat on a bench near the wall. I lay down on the bench. After a while Lidia appeared. She was wearing the strange dress she had worn on that Sunday morning with the lace at the shoulders and bosom. She asked me to make room and sat down close beside me. She put a hand on my shoulder. "My mother is an idiot. She's obsessed with those almonds," she said. She began to sigh, as she leaned against me, more and more heavily. "I shouldn't have married a vulgar man like Federico. I was in love with someone else, someone who had an education, someone like you'll be when you're grown up. They made me marry him, almost by force, because they didn't trust the other one," she said. She pressed against me. I felt her naked body under the light fabric. She took one of my hands and placed it on her breast. I breathed anxiously, afraid Federico would surprise us in that embrace. Guessing my thought Lidia said, "Don't worry, my husband is in bed and at this hour he's already asleep." She added, "I'm sorry. I have to vent with someone now that Lena's not around." I imagined mysterious, merciless relations between Lidia and Lena, and an abyss opened before me. I fled to my room, leaving Lidia alone in the garden. I went to the window, and for a long time listened to the woman walking on the gravel, now closer, now farther away. That night I couldn't sleep. I would have liked to see Lena at least once. The next day my mother arrived. Mauro had gone on business to a distant city. No one, although they treated me coldly, spoke to my mother about the almonds and Lidia's underwear.

Sandra and Federico seemed to have forgotten everything, in fact Sandra invited mamma to stay a few days more. We said goodbye and departed. Mamma said it was our duty to say goodbye to Mauro, too, who had returned from his business trip and now was in his shop, which was right on the street that led to the station. We drove there in a carriage. I was relaxed, now that I had left the house of Sandra, Antonio, Federico, Lidia, and the mysterious presence of Lena. My mother asked the driver to wait for us. We got out of the carriage and went into a big room filled with bolts of cloth. Mauro was leaning on a counter. He embraced my mother. But he didn't shake the hand I held out to him. "He did well on his exams. It may be my impression, but it seems to me that in recent days he's also grown in height," mamma said. "Weeds always grow," Mauro said sharply. "Did they tell you what this filthy pig did in my house?" I felt myself turning red. The persecution against me, ceaseless and unjust, continued. I hugged my mother and started to cry. And I wept for the innocence I believed I had lost, for the chill that, thanks to Sandra's family, walled me in, and, behind that chill, for what was going to happen to me. My mother pushed me away, looking at me with revulsion from head to foot. On the table were some big scissors. I made as if to grab them: I wanted to hit Mauro. He blocked my path. He offered his hand to my mother and said, ironically, "Go, signora, don't keep the carriage waiting."

AFTERWORD

The Impossible and the Eternal

In Rome recently, I saw a small show of works by Fra Angelico. The magic of his paintings and frescoes has endured from the fifteenth century to the present. Over time, of course, our perception and our comprehension of the pictures changes, perhaps the very code by which to interpret them has been lost, and yet confronted by those Madonnas and angels, those crucifixes, we are astonished, and continue to prize their mysterious beauty.

Why read *The Chill* today? Why read an author like Bilenchi?

For at least four important reasons: the first is his choice of adolescent protagonists. Every era writes and updates its own coming-of-age novel, but the narrative of adolescence is an archetype, a symbolic primal phase, and there are writers who, like Bilenchi, remain focused on that stage for their whole life. From *Anna and Bruno* (1938) and *The Conservatory of St. Teresa* (1940) to the stories *The Drought* (1940) and *Poverty* (1941), joined, forty years later, by *The Chill* (1982)—to complete the triptych *The Impossible Years* (1984)—Bilenchi writes a single, continuous novel of childhood and adolescence, of which *The Chill* is a perfect miniature, the apex and culmination. In this he resembles J.D. Salinger and Henry Roth, great

American writers who, in their fiction, examine this turbulent and impossible period of our life, as the Italian Elsa Morante does in *Arturo's Island*. The choice of the coming-of-age story, of adolescent characters caught in the web of an endless present, guarantees the freedom of continuing to exist, in spite of and beyond history.

Hence the second reason to read *The Chill*, which is political and civil: freedom from any ideology and from the limits imposed by history. In Bilenchi's stories there is freedom, and so we train our capacity to be and remain free; and this, yesterday and today, in Italy and in the United States, is no small thing.

The third reason is the Italian landscape, central in all Bilenchi's narratives, a landscape that comes to meet us like a real character, a geography that barely survives up and down the Italian boot but that still endures in the Tuscany of our time.

Bilenchi manages to perform the miracle of reviving indigenous elements of Italian culture "naturally," and history, reduced to background, to outline, gives way to elemental, immutable forms of existence: the house, the hills, the plain, the river, the clay hills, the sunflower field, the street. It's an Italian landscape, invented and remembered, of turreted cities, castles, abbeys, and countryside that is the symbolic correlative of the unfolding of consciousness: "Once I had stepped out of our front door, Via dei Tre Mori gave me the right thrust toward time. The façades, one against the next, gray, green, pink, ochre, inspired a peaceful, light serenity and pleasure, heightened by the green that I could see in the distance, touching the sky."

The fourth and final reason to read *The Chill* has to do with Bilenchi's language, a simple, denotative, anti-rhetorical language, along with a paratactic style that leads the reader to within a millimeter of the things that are described, and that Ann Goldstein has successfully brought to life in her translation of this long story.

And there is something else: what remains in any mathematical equation whose solution is a repeating decimal. That incalculable, impossible, inexpressible remainder is what literature is engaged with. It's ultimately the reason that we remain imprisoned in the pages of a book. The meaning of literature is not the achievement, the flag, the proclamation or edict—that is not the meaning of literature. Literature is the open wound, the sore, the shadow, the night; it offers a thousand questions and the trajectory of a thousand possible answers. All Bilenchi's fiction is marked by this fact, and that is why it endures. That is also why we continue to read him.

In the early eighties, Romano Bilenchi, born in 1909, and the undisputed master of the Italian short story, worked on a draft of *The Chill*, returning through the filter of memory to the period between adolescence and the threshold of maturity. His long fidelity to his themes (the mother-son relationship, friendship, love, death, hatred, revenge, the landscape) indicates the focus of his inspiration on the *incipient man* and the perfect reflection of his writing in a narrative universe organized by strongly self-referential paradigms. "Childhood interests me because those are the years when a man is shaped," Bilenchi said. "Man interests me when he's born and when he dies, that's why I've often written about adolescence: adolescence is a poetic invention, it's like the first person, an extra invention, an extra fact that enters the story. The most disturbing moment is the present, the time of change, the instant when something has to happen."

In Bilenchi's fiction nothing happens that is not life itself, life as childhood. Through the lens of childhood and adolescence he captures the flow of existence, in its endless movement and constant change: as if catching a wave at the instant of greatest extension, where anything can still happen. His stories are stories in suspension, stories of waiting, stories of destiny, where the imprint of destiny is in the present that is about to be fulfilled.

"I work on words, choosing those which for me, at a given moment, have the greatest poetic resonance. 'Chill,' for example, which provides the title for the last story I wrote, in 1981, is a word that stuck in my mind for years, and at a certain point, after ten years during which I wrote nothing, I began to develop it into a theme. Everything is in the first lines of the story: 'The chill of suspicion and incomprehension arose between me and men when I was sixteen, at the time of my high-school exams'; otherwise the events or the plot come by themselves, it's enough to know how to look for them."

The protagonist's story is wound tight around the theme of the chill and unfolds without a real beginning or end, without redemption and without salvation, fixed on that note. *The Chill* is narrated in the first person, and the point of view is strictly that of an adolescent during the painful passage to adulthood. The whole story is filtered through the young gaze of the I-protagonist, and it moves with the very flow of life, halting before the incomprehensibility of becoming an adult. Bilenchi's nihilism is gentle but inexorable, that of a man who has sought positive and progressive achievements in his life and has emerged defeated. Now his words take the same journey and return to their destiny of frustration and loss.

"The problem of developing this word 'chill' obsessed me for ten years. Let's say like a kind of symphony, one of those very repetitive pieces of music, like a bolero." Here is the theme of the bolero, the aimless movement of knowledge, the repetitive music of every journey to maturity: "Words are like stones that you throw in a pool of water, producing wider and wider concentric circles." Childhood as the real, as what exceeds reality, contains it and goes beyond it, a glass bubble that holds everything and from which you cannot get out: "until the anxiety vanished, leaving me in a room that did not belong to any house, that was not in any place on earth."

The death of the grandfather while the boy is on an outing to the castle and the abbey is the first sign of painful separation from the world of childhood: "It was in grandfather's company that I had conceived my first thoughts of death, had begun to meditate on the mystery of it and the various ways we can meet it on our path." This memory of going with his grandfather to visit a friend who is the director of a museum in a neighboring city, the inspection of the excavations, and the chance finding of the statue of an athlete and, under it, a leather purse full of ancient Roman coins, initiates a series of reflections on the precariousness of existence, on the value of precariousness and the possibility of leaving some trace of our passage.

Echoing in intensity the meditation on death is the episode of the boy's initiation into sexuality in the sunflower field: "The sunflowers also seemed to be living, insidious beings who, for mysterious reasons, offered the hornets shelter and rich, exciting nourishment." Gino, the

son of a farmer, will become the go-between for the discovery of sex: "One day he told me that he was a friend of
the hornets and the sunflowers and always brought them
some little beast to eat that he had killed with the pruning
knife." And Gino's words about Vera, the young protagonist's cousin, dazzle him: "I've seen her sex. She always sits
on the stairs with her legs spread. She has a pink sex, it
looks like a clean wound. Sometimes I feel like bringing
her here, then sticking the tip of the pruning knife into her,
ripping her apart like a guinea pig, and leaving her to the
hornets." These are implacable images, where nature takes
the upper hand and is revealed in its bare cruelty—images
that are indelible in the reader's mind.

The adolescent protagonists of Bilenchi's stories are
creatures haunted by the childhood of the world, their
development necessarily failed; they live not in history but
in eternity, untouched by the repose of maturity because
they are in constant motion, with the unceasing pulse of
feeling themselves alive. They are creatures who belong to
the eternity of existence, to the timeless island of childhood and adolescence, not the one that is lost but the one
that persists in every beginning. These adolescent protagonists are prisoners of desire, of what must happen but
whose actual happening does not matter, because it is
there that that motionless movement finds its home, the
possibility of inventing and recounting life as it extends
outward and then condenses. Writing about childhood
renders visible the very mechanism of writing, engaged not
with reality but with the real: childhood as the mental
place of poetic creation, as the engine of narration, as a
creative fantasy "capable on the slightest pretext of trans-

forming our small garden into an immense forest populated by elephants, equatorial birds, fierce beasts."

In Bilenchi writer and narrator coincide; the construction of consciousness advances by trial and error, and gradually takes shape through juxtapositions, tugs, tears: love and jealousy, friendship and betrayal, joy and suffering, happiness and sorrow. Prevailing over all is the complex, multiform, vague, and rarefied representation of the formation of consciousness. Bilenchi's characters proceed with eyes closed, the only possible exploratory method for a narrator who wants to obscure the portrayal of things rather than give it definition. The author works on dissolving the character, on pulverizing it, constructing complex systems of drives and affects, while the words return to their origin, to an elemental, primal scansion. The language and syntax contract to the essential, to the difficult syllabification of consciousness, becoming as vital as breathing, as the involuntary beating of the heart.

Bilenchi is a narrator of the threshold, the boundary, his is a world of epiphanies, of flashes that are the prelude to an event, to something inexpressible that wants urgently to be said. His faithfulness to poetry is a necessity; his writing works under the surface of consciousness to make what he wants to say emerge from the depths, without the language of the profound. Bilenchi's stories seem touched by grace; they control a complex and changing narrative material where myth and reality meet in the enchanted space of adolescence, a space marked by situations and events that are not chronological or historical but that become a metronome of consciousness, an internal tempo formed by affective relations. In Bilenchi's continuous and, as the critic Mario Luzi has put it, "consubstantial" novel about the narrow passage from adolescent to adult, history is erased, to re-emerge in tiny daily events, so internal that history is hurled into the mouth of the volcano, reduced to lava and ashes. Man and history derive from discontinuity and from randomness.

Nothing was more congenial to this writer of the impossible, a passionate reader of European and American literature and firmly anchored in the oldest Italian tradition. Bilenchi is an author who instinctively has the characteristics of the classical, and knows what expressionism is, but who, because of his own internal stylistic order or because of his neurotic passion for revising, chooses the cleanness of form, the essential geometry of syntax, clarity, transparency achieved by paring down, and through endless successive rewritings. The result is narratives whose surfaces are translucent like those of the predellas under the imposing altarpieces of Giotto or Fra Angelico.

Benedetta Centovalli
June, 2009

ABOUT THE AUTHOR

Romano Bilenchi was born in Colle di Val d'Elsa, between Florence and Siena, on November 9, 1909. His passion for literature developed during his school years in Colle. He attended high school in Florence, and there, in 1930, he met the writer and novelist Elio Vittorini—the start of a lifelong friendship. He began contributing to the journals *Selvaggio* and *Universale*, for which he wrote both stories and political pieces. He also contributed stories and articles to *Bargello* and *Critica fascista*. Although as a young man Bilenchi subscribed to what was later called "Fascism of the left" (which emphasized the anti-bourgeois and revolutionary aspect of Fascism), he was increasingly critical, and along with other intellectuals, eventually arriving at a progressive and radical change of position. During that period, he published his first two books, *Vita di Pisto* ("The Life of Pisto"), in 1931, and *Storia dei socialisti di Colle* ("History of the Socialists of Colle"), in 1933, both of which he later rejected as *strapaesane*, that is, tied to local, rural revolutionary ideals, in contrast to the cosmopolitan outlook of other Italian intellectuals. At that time, too, he established a close friendship with the painter Ottone Rosai.

From 1934 to 1943, Bilenchi worked at the daily *La Nazione,* in Florence, at the time a flourishing cultural capital. Moving to the city, he frequented the Giubbe Rosse, the Paszkowski, and the Caffè San Marco, meeting places for writers and artists from Montale to Landolfi and Gadda. He became friends in particular with the poet Mario Luzi and the novelist Vasco Pratolini.

In 1935, he published *Il capofabbrica* ("The Factory Manager") and began contributing to the journal *Letteratura*. The story collection *Anna e Bruno* ("Anna and Bruno") came out in 1938, and addresses themes of childhood and adolescence that came to be central in all his fiction. By this time, his doubts about Fascism had reached a decisive point, and he became an active supporter of the clandestine Communist Party.

In 1940 he published the novel *Il Conservatorio di Santa Teresa* ("The Conservatory of Santa Teresa"), which marked a turning point in his fiction. *La siccità* ("The Drought") and *La miseria* ("Poverty") followed, in 1940 and 1941.

In 1942 Bilenchi joined the Italian Communist Party and took part in the Florentine resistance. After the war he became the editor-in-chief of the *Nuovo Corriere*, a Florentine daily with a national circulation, which—although it was supported by the Party—established itself as a free workshop of ideas and analyses, reports and reflections, welcoming the most important names in the city and in the country. After the paper took a stand against the repression of the popular uprisings in Poznán, Poland, in 1956, its Party financing was suspended and it was forced to close.

Bilenchi left the Communist Party in 1957 and returned to *La Nazione* as the editor of the cultural pages, and he remained there until 1971, the year he retired.

In 1972 he published *Il bottone di Stalingrado* ("The Button of Stalingrad"), a novel that assessed recent Italian history from the birth of Fascism to the early postwar period. (It won the Viareggio prize.)

The memoir *Amici: Vittorini, Rosai e altri incontri* ("Friends: Vittorini, Rosai and Other Encounters"), in 1976, marked a new creative season (a second version of *Friends* came out in 1988 and a third, posthumously, in 1990). *Il gelo* ("The Chill") appeared in 1982 and in 1984 it completed, with *La siccità* ("The Drought") and *La miseria* ("Poverty,") the trilogy *Gli anni impossibili* ("The Impossible Years").

Bilenchi died in Florence, on November 18, 1989, a week after his eightieth birthday.

Carmine Abate
Between Two Seas
"A moving portrayal of generational continuity."—*Kirkus*
192 pp • $14.95 • 978-1-933372-40-2

Salwa Al Neimi
The Proof of the Honey
"Al Neimi announces the end of a taboo in the Arab world: that of sex!"—*Reuters*
160 pp • $15.00 • 978-1-933372-68-6

Alberto Angela
A Day in the Life of Ancient Rome
"Fascinating and accessible."—*Il Giornale*
392 pp • $16.00 • 978-1-933372-71-6

Muriel Barbery
The Elegance of the Hedgehog
"Gently satirical, exceptionally winning and inevitably bittersweet."—Michael Dirda, *The Washington Post*
336 pp • $15.00 • 978-1-933372-60-0

Stefano Benni
Margherita Dolce Vita
"A modern fable...hilarious social commentary."—*People*
240 pp • $14.95 • 978-1-933372-20-4

Timeskipper
"Benni again unveils his Italian brand of magical realism."
—*Library Journal*
400 pp • $16.95 • 978-1-933372-44-0

Massimo Carlotto
The Goodbye Kiss
"A masterpiece of Italian noir."—*Globe and Mail*
160 pp • $14.95 • 978-1-933372-05-1

Death's Dark Abyss
"A remarkable study of corruption and redemption."
—*Kirkus* (starred review)
160 pp • $14.95 • 978-1-933372-18-1

The Fugitive
"[Carlotto is] the reigning king of Mediterranean noir."
—*The Boston Phoenix*
176 pp • $14.95 • 978-1-933372-25-9

www.europaeditions.com

Francisco Coloane
Tierra del Fuego
"Coloane is the Jack London of our times."
—Alvaro Mutis
176 pp • $14.95 • 978-1-933372-63-1

Giancarlo De Cataldo
The Father and the Foreigner
"A slim but touching noir novel from one of Italy's best writers
in the genre."—*Quaderni Noir*
160 pp • $15.00 • 978-1-933372-72-3

Shashi Deshpande
The Dark Holds No Terrors
"[Deshpande is] an extremely talented storyteller."
—*Hindustan Times*
272 pp • $15.00 • 978-1-933372-67-9

Steve Erickson
Zeroville
"A funny, disturbing, daring and demanding novel—Erickson's
best."
—*The New York Times Book Review*
352 pp • $14.95 • 978-1-933372-39-6

Elena Ferrante
The Days of Abandonment
"The raging, torrential voice of [this] author is something rare."
—The New York Times
192 pp • $14.95 • 978-1-933372-00-6

Troubling Love
"Ferrante's polished language belies the rawness of her imagery."
—The New Yorker
144 pp • $14.95 • 978-1-933372-16-7

The Lost Daughter
"So refined, almost translucent."
—The Boston Globe
144 pp • $14.95 • 978-1-933372-42-6

Jane Gardam
Old Filth
"Old Filth belongs in the Dickensian pantheon
of memorable characters."
—*The New York Times Book Review*
304 pp • $14.95 • 978-1-933372-13-6

The Queen of the Tambourine
"A truly superb and moving novel."
—*The Boston Globe*
272 pp • $14.95 • 978-1-933372-36-5

The People on Privilege Hill
"Engrossing stories of hilarity and heartbreak."
—*Seattle Times*
208 pp • $15.95 • 978-1-933372-56-3

Alicia Giménez-Bartlett
Dog Day
"Delicado and Garzón prove to be one of the more engaging
sleuth teams to debut in a long time."
—*The Washington Post*
320 pp • $14.95 • 978-1-933372-14-3

Prime Time Suspect
"A gripping police procedural."
—*The Washington Post*
320 pp • $14.95 • 978-1-933372-31-0

Death Rites
"Petra is developing into a good cop, and her earnest efforts
to assert her authority…are worth cheering."
—*The New York Times*
304 pp • $16.95 • 978-1-933372-54-9

Katharina Hacker
The Have-Nots
"Hacker's prose soars."
—*Publishers Weekly*
352 pp • $14.95 • 978-1-933372-41-9

Patrick Hamilton
Hangover Square
"Patrick Hamilton's novels are dark tunnels of misery,
loneliness, deceit, and sexual obsession."
—*New York Review of Books*
336 pp • $14.95 • 978-1-933372-06-8

James Hamilton-Paterson
Cooking with Fernet Branca
"Irresistible!"
—*The Washington Post*
288 pp • $14.95 • 978-1-933372-01-3

Amazing Disgrace
"It's loads of fun, light and dazzling as a peacock feather."
—*New York Magazine*
352 pp • $14.95 • 978-1-933372-19-8

Rancid Pansies
"Campy comic saga about hack writer and self-styled
'culinary genius' Gerald Samper."
—*Seattle Times*
288 pp • $15.95 • 978-1-933372-62-4

Seven-Tenths: The Sea and Its Thresholds
"The kind of book that, were he alive now, Shelley
might have written."
—Charles Sprawson
416 pp • $16.00 • 978-1-933372-69-3

Alfred Hayes
The Girl on the Via Flaminia
"Immensely readable."
—*The New York Times*
160 pp • $14.95 • 978-1-933372-24-2

Jean-Claude Izzo
Total Chaos
"Izzo's Marseilles is ravishing."—*Globe and Mail*
256 pp • $14.95 • 978-1-933372-04-4

Chourmo
"A bitter, sad and tender salute to a place equally impossible
to love or leave."—*Kirkus* (starred review)
256 pp • $14.95 • 978-1-933372-17-4

Solea
"[Izzo is] a talented writer who draws from the deep,
dark well of noir."—*The Washington Post*
208 pp • $14.95 • 978-1-933372-30-3

The Lost Sailors
"Izzo digs deep into what makes men weep."
—*Time Out New York*
272 pp • $14.95 • 978-1-933372-35-8

A Sun for the Dying
"Beautiful, like a black sun, tragic and desperate."—*Le Point*
224 pp • $15.00 • 978-1-933372-59-4

Gail Jones
Sorry
"Jones's gift for conjuring place and mood rarely falters."
—*Times Literary Supplement*
240 pp • $15.95 • 978-1-933372-55-6

Matthew F. Jones
Boot Tracks
"A gritty action tale."
—*The Philadelphia Inquirer*
208 pp • $14.95 • 978-1-933372-11-2

Ioanna Karystiani
The Jasmine Isle
"A modern Greek tragedy about love foredoomed
and family life."
—*Kirkus*
288 pp • $14.95 • 978-1-933372-10-5

Gene Kerrigan
The Midnight Choir
"The lethal precision of his closing punches leave
quite a lasting mark."
—*Entertainment Weekly*
368 pp • $14.95 • 978-1-933372-26-6

Little Criminals
"A great story…relentless and brilliant."
—Roddy Doyle
352 pp • $16.95 • 978-1-933372-43-3

Peter Kocan
Fresh Fields
"A stark, harrowing, yet deeply courageous work of immense
power and magnitude."—*Quadrant*
304 pp • $14.95 • 978-1-933372-29-7

The Treatment and the Cure
"Kocan tells this story with grace and humor."
—*Publishers Weekly*
256 pp • $15.95 • 978-1-933372-45-7

Helmut Krausser
Eros
"Helmut Krausser has succeeded in writing a great German epochal novel."
—*Focus*
352 pp • $16.95 • 978-1-933372-58-7

Amara Lakhous
Clash of Civilizations Over an Elevator in Piazza Vittorio
"Do we have an Italian Camus on our hands? Just possibly."
—*The Philadelphia Inquirer*
144 pp • $14.95 • 978-1-933372-61-7

Carlo Lucarelli
Carte Blanche
"Lucarelli proves that the dark and sinister are better evoked
when one opts for unadulterated grit and grime."
—*The San Diego Union-Tribune*
128 pp • $14.95 • 978-1-933372-15-0

The Damned Season
"De Luca...is a man both pursuing and pursued. And that makes
him one of the more interesting figures in crime fiction."
—*The Philadelphia Inquirer*
128 pp • $14.95 • 978-1-933372-27-3

Via delle Oche
"Delivers a resolution true to the series' moral relativism."
—*Publishers Weekly*
160 pp • $14.95 • 978-1-933372-53-2

www.europaeditions.com

Edna Mazya
Love Burns
"Combines the suspense of a murder mystery with the absurdity
of a Woody Allen movie."
—*Kirkus*
224 pp • $14.95 • 978-1-933372-08-2

Sélim Nassib
I Loved You for Your Voice
"Nassib spins a rhapsodic narrative out of the indissoluble
connection between two creative souls."
—*Kirkus*
272 pp • $14.95 • 978-1-933372-07-5

The Palestinian Lover
"A delicate, passionate novel in which history and life are
inextricably entwined."
—*RAI Books*
192 pp • $14.95 • 978-1-933372-23-5

Amélie Nothomb
Tokyo Fiancée
"Intimate and honest...depicts perfectly a nontraditional romance."
—*Publishers Weekly*
160 pp • $15.00 • 978-1-933372-64-8

Alessandro Piperno
The Worst Intentions
"A coruscating mixture of satire, family epic, Proustian meditation, and erotomaniacal farce."
—*The New Yorker*
320 pp • $14.95 • 978-1-933372-33-4

Eric-Emmanuel Schmitt
The Most Beautiful Book in the World
"Nine novellas, parables on the idea of a future, filled with redeeming optimism."
—*Lire Magazine*
192 pp • $15.00 • 978-1-933372-74-7

Domenico Starnone
First Execution
"Starnone's books are small theatres of action, both physical and psychological."
—*L'espresso* (Italy)
176 pp • $15.00 • 978-1-933372-66-2

Joel Stone
The Jerusalem File
"Joel Stone is a major new talent."
—*Cleveland Plain Dealer*
160 pp • $15.00 • 978-1-933372-65-5

Benjamin Tammuz
Minotaur
"A novel about the expectations and compromises that humans create for themselves."
—*The New York Times*
192 pp • $14.95 • 978-1-933372-02-0

Chad Taylor
Departure Lounge
"There's so much pleasure and bafflement to be derived
from this thriller."
—*The Chicago Tribune*
176 pp • $14.95 • 978-1-933372-09-9

Roma Tearne
Mosquito
"Vividly rendered...Wholly satisfying."
—*Kirkus*
352 pp • $16.95 • 978-1-933372-57-0

Bone China
"Tearne deftly reveals the corrosive effects of civil strife
on private lives and the redemptiveness of art."
—*The Guardian*
432 pp • $16.00 • 978-1-933372-75-4

Christa Wolf
One Day a Year: 1960-2000
"Remarkable!"
—*The New Yorker*
640 pp • $16.95 • 978-1-933372-22-8

Edwin M. Yoder Jr.
Lions at Lamb House
"Yoder writes with such wonderful manners, learning, and detachment."
—William F. Buckley, Jr.
256 pp • $14.95 • 978-1-933372-34-1

Michele Zackheim
Broken Colors
"A beautiful novel."
—*Library Journal*
320 pp • $14.95 • 978-1-933372-37-2